CLAIMED BY HER MATES

GRACE GOODWIN

Published by Stormy Night Publications and Design, LLC.
www.StormyNightPublications.com

Cover design by Korey Mae Johnson
www.koreymaejohnson.com

Images by Period Images, 123RF/Dmitriy Denysov, and
123RF/blueskyimage

1st Print Edition. May 2016

ISBN-13: 978-1533072214

ISBN-10: 1533072213

CHAPTER ONE

Leah

I tried to fight the feelings. I truly did, but the cock filling me up just felt too good. I even tried to fight *him*, but all it got me was a set of leather cuffs around my wrists. I was on my hands and knees, my body pressed against a strange, padded table. My cuffs were linked to the rings set low so I could not move. I tugged once, twice, but there was no give. My ass tilted high in the air, my mate's cock deep inside me. It was like I was tied over an odd wooden horse while someone *rode* me. I was completely at his mercy and could do nothing but succumb to the power of his body as he took mine.

His cock might have been a part of him, flesh and blood—albeit very hard and very large—but he wielded it like a weapon designed to make me submit. Once he filled me with his seed, once his essence coated my inner walls, filled my womb, there would be no turning back. I would crave his touch and his taste. I would *need* him to fill me, to take me, to forever claim my body. Now, with him expertly stretching me wide, with my bare bottom burning from the sting of his hand and my pussy on fire from the touch of his

1

expert tongue, I didn't want to resist him any longer.

I used to be afraid. Now, I simply hungered. Ached.

He wasn't cruel; the opposite in fact. As my mate's cock moved inside me, filling me completely from behind before retreating, again and again, my fear left me. I was his now. He would own me, body and soul, but he was strong, a warrior. He would protect me. And fuck me. He would keep me in line with his firm hand, but also bring me pleasure, and safety, and a home. All these thoughts flooded my mind as this powerful male made me his forever, his cock invading my body over and over as I opened for him.

His large hands skimmed my back before he bent over, covering me with the heat of a warrior's strength, resting his fingers beside mine where I was cuffed to the table. The longer he took me, the tighter his grip became on the handles, the whiter the knuckles.

His slick chest lay over my back, pinning me against the bench, adding to the sensation of being trapped. I couldn't even avoid his harsh breathing, the sounds of pleasure that escaped his lips, for they were right by my ear.

"Feel that?" he growled, shifting his hips and hitting my womb with the hard tip of his cock. He was adept at stroking over secret, sensitive places deep inside that made my body quake, my mind blank, my submission complete. There was no one else who could make me feel this way. No one else had ever pushed my body to the brink of the most delicious pleasure.

As I was positioned over the bench, my breasts hung down and ached to be touched. My clit was swollen and if he even brushed over it with just the tip of his finger, I would come. But he would deny me for now. He would deny me until I broke, until I begged.

I couldn't help the breathy "Yes" that escaped my lips. I could hear the wet sounds of fucking—the clearest sign of my arousal—fill the room.

"You feared my cock, but it only brings pleasure. I told you I'd fit, that we'd be perfect." He spoke as he fucked me.

How did he know my body so well when this was our first time? I'd never come from a cock before, only rubbing my clit in bed, alone. But now that personal task would be denied me. My mate insisted that I never come without permission again. If I broke this rule, I would be spanked long and hard. Now that I belonged to him, I would come by his will, by his tongue, his hand, his huge cock… or not at all.

"Your pleasure is mine."

"Yes," I replied.

"I feel you squeezing me."

"Yes," I cried, clenching down on him once again. It was all I could say for I had no control anymore. I was completely at his mercy and all I wanted to do was exactly what he demanded.

"You will not come until I give you permission." He lifted his hands from the table to stroke my breasts, the softest caress first, then a hard tug and pinching that made me whimper as he pounded into me hard and fast and deep. It was a pain/pleasure he elicited and I loved it. "You are mine. Your pussy is mine."

"Yes," I repeated, again and again.

He didn't stop riding me, fucking me, filling me, taking me. Claiming me. Higher and higher I climbed until I tossed my head back and forth and I gripped the handles with desperation so great I feared my heart would explode in my chest. I couldn't breathe. Couldn't think. Couldn't resist. I was there, right… there. My mate's hand skimmed my down my hip, roaming the softly rounded flesh of my body until he reached my clit. He traced the edges with his finger and the sound that left my throat was the soft scream of a creature in agony, frantic and lost. Nothing existed for me but his body, his voice, his breath, his touch.

"Come now," he commanded, his cock like a piston, his fingers on my clit hard and unforgiving.

My orgasm exploded deep within me, for I had no other choice. I couldn't resist it. I had no control. I was no longer myself, I was his. I screamed my release, my body clenching and releasing around his cock, pulling him in deeper, holding him all the way inside me. It was as if my body craved his life essence, was desperate for it.

My release triggered his and I felt him swell and grow even bigger before he growled in my ear, hot pulses of his seed filling me. My body greedily milked his cock of the life essence, taking it deep inside.

Just as he'd promised, something in his seed triggered a physical reaction in me, forcing me to come a second time.

"Yes, love. Yes, take every drop. Your body is changing. It knows me. It must have me. You will beg for my cock; you will crave my seed. You will need it, love it, just as I need and love you."

"Yes!" I cried again, knowing his words were true. It was a hot wash of pleasure that seeped through my body, directly from my pussy, then outward. He was right; now that I felt the power of him, of what he could give me, I was a slave to it. I was a slave to his cock.

"Miss Adams?"

"Yes," I said once again, my dream merging with the present.

"Miss Adams, your testing is over."

I shook my head. No. I was bound to a fucking bench and being fucked and filled with seed. I wanted to stay there. I wanted... more.

"Miss Adams!"

The voice was stern now, and loud. I forced my eyes open.

"Oh, God," I gasped, trying to catch my breath as my pussy clenched and pulsed with aftershocks of my orgasms. I wasn't tied down to a fucking bench. No solid male body pressed into my back. I was in the Interstellar Bride Program's processing center in a medical examination gown. My wrists were trapped in medical restraints secured to the edges of an uncomfortable reclining chair, similar to a dentist's, for the last stage of preparations for going off-planet. I hadn't realized, when they'd hooked up the wires and sensors, that I would end up in a sex dream. I felt the lingering effects of it. My pussy was wet, the back of my scratchy medical gown damp. My nipples were hard and my hands were clenched into fists. I felt wrung out and used. I felt complete.

"As I said, your testing is over." Warden Egara stood before me. A stern young woman with dark brown hair and a hawk-like attention to every detail of the matching process, she glanced down at her tablet as her finger ran over it. "Your match has been made."

I licked my dry lips as I tried to slow my frantic heart. Goosebumps broke out on my sweaty skin. "The dream… was it real?"

"It wasn't a dream," she replied, her tone matter-of-fact. "We use recorded sensory data from prior brides to assist in the matching process."

"What?" Recorded data?

"A neuro-processing unit, or NPU, will be inserted in your skull before you leave Earth. It assists in language and helps you adapt to your new world." She grinned then, and the sight was as frightening as it was wicked. "The NPU is programmed to record your mating and send the data back to the system."

"You are going to record me with my new mate?"

"Yes. That is required by the matching protocol. All claiming ceremonies are reviewed to ensure that our brides are safely and properly placed." She dropped the tablet to her side and I noticed the stiff collar and starched skirt of her uniform. There was not a wrinkle to be seen, not a single hair out of place in her tight chignon. She looked almost like a robot. But the fire in her eyes betrayed her fervor and dedication to her duty. Her devotion to the program was clearly evident in her next words. "We do all we can to make sure our warriors receive worthy brides. They serve us all, protecting the Earth and all member planets from certain destruction. The system uses your body's reactions to probe your inner conscience, your darkest fantasies, your innermost needs. What didn't interest you was quickly discarded by the matching program. The sensory input was filtered until we found a warrior from a planet with a perfect match."

That had been my match? Surely not. "I can't be matched to a man who ties me up. That's not what I wanted when I volunteered."

Her dark eyebrow winged up at that. "Apparently, Miss Adams, that is exactly what you desire. The testing reveals the truth, even if your mind denies it."

I thought of her words as she moved around the table and took a seat opposite me. Her crisp uniform for the Interstellar Bride Program matched her cool demeanor. "You are an unusual case, Miss Adams. While we do have a few volunteers, we have never had one with your reasons before."

I glanced at the closed door for a moment, worried that perhaps she'd called my fiancé and had sent for him. Sheer panic had me tugging at the restraints.

"Do not worry," she said, her one hand raised to stop me. "You are safe here. While you've stated that the bruises on your body are from a fall, I felt it necessary to ensure that no one be allowed to see you before I send you off-planet."

Obviously Warden Egara didn't believe my ridiculous story, and I was reassured by her vehemence in protecting me. I'd never skied in my life. I didn't even live anywhere near a mountain, but a reasonable excuse was required for the bruises on my body and it was the first thing that came to mind.

While I'd assumed the bruises would be uncovered, I'd had no idea that I would be stripped bare for medical tests, then placed in a hospital gown and put through a screening of completely inappropriate images and motion clips. I must have fallen asleep, for I could not have imagined any of it on my own.

"Thank you," I replied.

I wasn't used to people being kind. She remained quiet as if waiting for me to tell her the truth. Did I want to share what I knew now about my fiancé? He'd been so kind, sweeping me off my feet, until I learned the truth. I'd overheard him telling one of his men to kill someone who had made one of his real estate deals fall through. I'd thought the men he kept around were employees, bodyguards, but they were enforcers, men he used to intimidate and kill. Once I'd agreed to marry him, he'd assigned two of his men as my personal *bodyguards*. Even then I'd believed the reason was simply that he was rich and I needed extra protection. I'd thought him considerate and caring, watching out for me. Ha! I'd been so *stupid*. Even more stupid when I told him I was having second thoughts about our wedding. He'd gone ballistic, grabbed me and told me he was never letting me go. Never.

When I threatened to leave, he quietly and fervently explained that he owned me. I was his property as soon as I'd placed his engagement ring on my finger. He'd kill anyone I kissed, torture any man who touched me, and then punish me for the trouble.

I knew then I had to get away, but I'd have to find a way to escape. I'd gone to the mall in my car as if it were a normal day. The men who watched me always parked their car beside mine, followed me through the mall, but allowed me to roam inside the stores alone. Just in case, I veered directly for the lingerie department where I knew they always backed off, then weaved through several other stores, dropping my cell phone between two racks of clothes. I hurried to the bus stop and took the bus across town. From there I'd hired a taxi to the Interstellar Bride Program's processing center.

I had no family, no friends left. When we'd begun dating he'd systematically removed everyone from my life I had cared about before I met him. One by one, he'd offered reasons for why they were no longer appropriate, no longer acceptable contacts. I was totally and completely alone in the world now, at his mercy. He'd even convinced me to give up my job, so I had no money of my own.

God help me, but even an alien was better than a psychotic, possessive man whose idea of punishment involved boxing practice, with me as the punching bag. I'd suffered it once. Never again. I might have been foolish, naïve, and even a little love-struck, but no longer.

I'd looked over my shoulder the entire trip to the processing center, afraid they'd track me down and stop me before I could enter the building. Once within the walls I felt safer, but I wouldn't feel completely out of their reach until I was off-planet. Only then would I breathe easy, confident that my fiancé could never find me.

I'd heard about the Interstellar Bride Program for over a year, knowing that most women who participated were prisoners seeking an alternative to a harsh prison sentence. Some, I'd learned, were volunteers, but none could return. Once matched to an alien warrior and sent off-planet to their mate, they were no longer citizens of Earth and could not return. At first, it had sounded scary and ridiculous. Who would *volunteer* to leave Earth? How bad could their lives be to do such a thing? Now I knew. A woman's life could turn very, *very* bad.

I needed to be as far away from my fiancé as possible and I worried that there would be no place on Earth that would be far enough. He would find me, then...

I'd thought he would be my family. *Family.* He'd chosen me to be his wife because I had none. I had no ties, no one to protect me, to keep me from marrying the asshole. He would never be my family. No one on Earth held any love for me. As a volunteer of the bride program, I was glad to know I couldn't return. I didn't want to be on Earth any longer. I didn't want to have the fear of him hunting me lingering for the remainder of my life. And so I would go off-planet, to the only place he could never find me, never reach me again.

And so here I sat, in a scratchy gown, under the scrutiny

of Warden Egara.

"Do you have questions?"

I licked my lips again. "This match... how do I know he will be... nice?" While I'd been put through so many tests for the matching, my only requirement was that he was nice. I didn't want to be mated to a man who beat me. If I wanted that, I could just stay here on Earth and marry the asshole.

"Nice? Miss Adams, I believe I understand the depth of your concern, but your mate has been put through the same tests. In fact, the warriors are required to submit to more advanced testing than our brides. You do not need to fear your match, for your subconscious minds are what determine a match. Your needs and desires complement one another. However, you must remember, a different planet has different customs. A different culture. You will need to adjust to this, to reject your Earthly judgments and antiquated notions. You will need to set aside your fear of men. Leave them here on Earth."

The words were wise, but the deed not so easily done. I would be cautious for a long time, I was sure. "Where am I going?"

"Viken."

I frowned. "I've never heard of the planet."

"Mmm," she replied, looking down at her table. "You are the first from Earth to be matched there. The dreams you saw were a female from another planet and her matched Viken. As you saw, he was an attentive, yet thorough lover."

I blushed at the memory.

"Based on this testing, I think you will be very pleased with your mate."

"And if I'm not?" What if she was wrong and he was mean? He might be able to wield his cock like porn star, but what if he wanted me to be nothing more than a slave to him? What if he beat me like my fiancé did?

"You have thirty days to change your mind," she answered. "Keep in mind you have been matched not only to a man, but to the planet. If you do not find your match

9

acceptable after thirty days, you may request another warrior, but you will remain on Viken."

That seemed reasonable. I sighed, relaxing at the notion that I could make my own choice in the end—and not be sent back to Earth.

"You are satisfied?" she asked. "Do you have more questions? Is there any reason to delay your transport?"

She looked to me as if offering me one last opportunity. An opportunity I would not take. "No. There is no reason to delay."

She nodded her head. "Very good. For the record, Miss Adams, are you married?"

"No." If I hadn't gotten away, I would have been. In two weeks.

"Do you have any children?"

"No."

"Good." She swiped her screen again. "You have been formally matched to the planet Viken. Do you accept the match?"

"Yes," I replied. As long as the man wasn't mean, I would go anywhere to escape.

"Because of your affirmative response, you have been officially matched and are now stripped of your citizenship of Earth. You are now, and will forever be, a bride of Viken." She glanced down at her screen, swiped her finger over it. "Per Viken custom, some modifications to your body are required before your transport."

Warden Egara stood and came around beside me.

"Modifications?" What did that mean? What was she going to do?

She pushed a button on the wall above my head, which made it slide open. Glancing over my shoulder, I couldn't see more than soft blue lighting. What I did notice was the large arm that extended out from the wall with a needle attached. "What's that?"

"No need to be afraid. We are simply implanting your NPU, required for all brides. Hold still. It only takes a few seconds."

The robotic arm came toward me and poked into my neck. I winced at the surprise of it, but it didn't truly hurt. In fact, nothing hurt. As the chair moved backward into the room with the blue light, I was relaxed and calm, sleepy.

"You have nothing to fear any longer, Miss Adams." As the chair lowered into a warm bath, she added. "Your processing will begin in three… two… one."

CHAPTER TWO

Drogan

"We've spent almost thirty years apart. I do not see the need for us to come together now." I crossed my arms over my chest as I stared across the room at the two men who looked identical to me. My brothers. One had hair that was long, well past his shoulders, the other closely shorn with a scar through his right eyebrow, but otherwise it was like looking in a mirror. I'd known I was a triplet my entire life, known we'd been separated as babies. Even known the reason why.

"The Sector Wars happened when you were infants. After the death of your parents, it was decided to separate you. One child was sent to rule each of the three sectors in order to balance the power of your royal blood and end the war." Regent Bard looked between us. He was small and frail, but very powerful. We could have killed him easily with our bare hands, but we knew that his death would not change the course of events. I knew it, therefore bloodshed was useless. Since he was still breathing, my brothers must have come to the same conclusion. But none of us had to like it.

Standing next to the regent was his second-in-command, Gyndar. The regent only offered a simple introduction, but from all appearances, the man was to remain quiet and do the regent's bidding. He wasn't a young squire, green and eager, but an older man with a serious and calm demeanor. He was easily forgettable, which made him so very good at his job. My spies kept me informed of the regent's business, and Gyndar played a major role as an intermediary and negotiator, and quietly brokered agreements behind closed doors while Regent Bard kept up his public appearances and persona.

"We don't need a history lesson, regent. We are all aware that we were the reason the treaty was created, that the war ended," Tor said.

It was odd to hear my own voice come from someone else. His long hair and the heavier coat he wore were indications of his life in the colder Sector One. I'd never been there, of course, and had no interest in tolerating freezing weather.

"It was fortunate for you that we were triplets, wasn't it, regent?" Lev added. He moved to a high-backed chair, his short hair and fierce scowl somehow making him appear colder then Tor, but I knew that to be a misconception. Both of my brothers were hardened warriors, rulers of their sectors as I ruled mine. The fact that they'd survived these three decades was evidence of their strength and intelligence.

I could see similarities between myself and Lev. The way I, too, sat in a slouch with my long legs stretched out before me. I saw Lev's brow arch and, except for the scar, it was like looking in a reflecting glass. He also shared my disgust and disinterest in the maneuvering and scheming ways of politics. Neither brother was enjoying this meeting any more than I. It was an inconvenience, something we all had to tolerate.

The older man nodded. "It was fate, I believe, that your births brought peace to Viken."

I glanced at one brother, then the other, before I spoke. "And yet *we* have no peace. *We* are to mate a woman from another planet. *We* are to leave behind our homes, our people to live here, to live together and *share* a bride? You ask this after we have lived our entire lives in different sectors."

"We may have been born brothers, regent, but we are now enemies," Tor added. I nodded, as did Lev. I had no desire to leap across the room and murder my brothers, but my loyalty was to the people in my sector, as my brothers' loyalty was to the people in their own home sectors. We were born brothers in blood, but our loyalty belonged to our homes. To the people who we ruled. To the people who needed us to protect and provide for them.

"Enemies?" Regent Bard questioned. "No. Brothers. Identical brothers, with identical DNA, who will now claim one mate and breed her."

"So it is not us that you want." Lev steepled his fingers together. While he looked relaxed, I knew he was anything but. How I knew, I wasn't sure, but I could sense things in these two other men that I couldn't in others. Was it because we were triplets or was there some other way we had a bond? "It is the babe that we will make."

The old man didn't argue. "Yes. This child will unite the three sectors once again, become the ruler of all three. Equally. United. Together. Viken will once more come together under a single power, a single ruler. The wars will end once and for all."

"I, for one, do not desire an alien bride. If unity is your goal, we should claim a mate from Viken," Tor said, leaning against the wall of the room.

We were on Viken United, a small island with a handful of government buildings. This was the place all interstellar visitors arrived, where all formal meetings between sectors occurred. The giant white center building with its steep pinnacles and statues dedicated to all three sectors—the arrow, the sword, and the shield—was the one place considered neutral territory for all three sectors.

Weapons were left at the border. It was a safe area, a peaceful zone where tension could be resolved.

While the war had ended decades ago, animosity ran deep. Cultures varied. I disliked my brothers out of principle alone. I knew nothing about them besides what they looked like. Our bodies were identical, therefore I knew that Tor's cock angled to the left and Lev had a birthmark on his upper back. The rest, we were creatures of our people, creatures of our sectors.

"There is no Viken woman alive that can be truly neutral." He looked between the three of us. "Would you claim a mate from another sector?"

We each shook our head. It would be impossible to mate and fuck a woman from another sector. She would detest me and I would *tolerate* her. That was not the way of a mate and we all knew it. The bond had to be strong, powerful. Once mated, the connection was more powerful than anything else on Viken.

"Therefore, you have been mated to a woman off-planet. An Earth woman."

"Which one of us?" I asked. "Not all three of us are required for this. Surely one of my brothers knows enough about a woman to breed."

The men didn't argue with me. If they were anything like me, breeding a woman would not be a hardship or a problem.

"One is not sufficient." I swear Regent Bard paused for effect. "All of you must breed her. And it must be done within minutes of each other. You all must have an equal chance of siring the child."

The three of us glanced at each other, but said nothing. However, I knew what they were thinking. I couldn't *hear* their exact words, but I knew them just the same. "I don't share, regent. I'll take a bride, if you insist, but I will not share her."

"Then there will be war." At the regent's words Lev

shifted his stance and Tor's scowl deepened. "You three are the last of the royal bloodlines. The entire planet acknowledges your claim to the throne of Viken. You must claim a bride together. You must overcome your differences and lead your people to a new age of peace. We must stop fighting with each other and focus on the interstellar battle groups. We are no longer at liberty to fight amongst ourselves as children. The outside enemy draws near, and our warriors do not volunteer. Instead they stay home and raid one another's territory like spoiled children."

The regent took a deep breath, his rant one I'd heard many times. From the look on my brothers' faces, the regent's words were not new to them either. "You three are identical in every way. Your seed is identical, therefore any child from the mating union will represent all three of you, all three sectors."

"So we don't have to do this together," I said. "Either one of them can have the woman." I tilted my head in my brothers' direction.

As long as it wasn't me who ended up with the female. I didn't need one. Vikens treasured their females and children, but since I didn't have to worry about pleasing a woman, or taming one, life was so much simpler. When I wanted a woman in my bed, I took one. When I was done, she returned to her life as I returned to mine. I certainly didn't need to breed a female for any reason. Children meant devotion and a family, which I did not want. By all accounts, our parents had a loving mating, yet look where that got them. Dead. I didn't need to bring a woman to Viken and have her be killed for political reasons.

"I don't want a mate," Tor said. "He can have her." He pointed at Lev.

"Me? I don't want a mate."

The regent was so damn calm, so intent to set the planet to rights before his death. He *was* old and frail. Unlike the three of us, he'd witnessed a peaceful Viken. "It is done. She has been matched to all three of you. As Vikens, you know your responsibility."

Responsibility. That had been forced upon me from a very early age. There was responsibility to lead the planet, but not to breed a woman with my estranged brothers.

"We didn't ask for this," I said, speaking for my brothers as well. When they nodded, it was perhaps the first thing we'd ever agreed on.

"And will you all accept and name the child of your brother as your successor?"

"No." Lev's eyebrow arched again.

"Never." Tor's hands clenched into fists.

I did not respond, for my answer was the same. No. Never. I would never abandon my people to the offspring of another male. They were my people. My child would inherit the sacred mantle of leadership.

"And now you understand. You must all mate her." The regent raised his hand to silence me as I opened my mouth to argue. "You weren't asked to be born the three rulers of the planet. You didn't ask to be separated as infants. You were meant to be together, as one. You were born to rule, but your life has been, and will be, full of sacrifice. For the sake of the planet, for future generations, the feuding must end. Our warriors must once more rise in service to the Interstellar Coalition. We must protect our planet from the Hive, not fight amongst ourselves. If we do not once again meet our warrior quota, we will be removed from coalition protection. I received word that we have eighteen months to comply, to once more contribute to both the bride program and the warrior ranks, or Viken will be abandoned. I would see Viken unified and strong again. Protected. Proud. Before I die, we must restore Viken to its place as a powerful force in the fight against the Hive."

The Hive was a race of artificial beings that killed indiscriminately in their search for resources and new biological beings to assimilate into their collective. They took all free life forms and implanted them with technology, neuro-processors, and control mechanisms that stole a living creature's mind and soul. All member planets in the Interstellar Coalition contributed resources, ships, and warriors to the ongoing battle with the Hive and their indiscriminate evil.

The Hive had to be stopped. And the regent was correct. Viken had not sent its full quota of warriors, or brides, for many years. The thought that we might be abandoned had not occurred to me. The threat to the planet was real and unacceptable. Two solar cycles was barely enough time to breed a female and see the child born. Which meant we were truly out of time and out of options. I hated him for this, for telling us the truth. But I knew what must be done, no matter how much I didn't want to think of it.

"You have remained outside of the realm of interstellar politics and government, until now. Now, you must step up to the mantle and accept the responsibilities you were born to bear. All of Viken must be protected. We must be united. Viken must be strong. That is the truth, and it's the dream for which your parents sacrificed their lives."

Lev growled. "They *died* not because of peace, but because of war. The rebel factions hunted and murdered them in a bid for power. The Viken civil war ended because you split us up, not because you kept us together."

"You were babies then and could not yet rule," the regent added. "Now, now you have returned to Viken United, to the central sector of our planet to bring peace, not in a short-term measure, as your placement was, but forever. You three must put aside your differences and become a true united front. Together you will be powerful. Three brothers. One infant. One future."

"Fuck," Tor murmured. They were my sentiments as well. There was no escape from the regent's plan. There was no escape from the need to protect our people from both the Hive and the rebel factions on our own world. The rebels wanted a return to tribal ways, to a hundred different sectors, each with their own ruler, their own agenda. They wanted to return to the way Viken lived hundreds of years ago, before we became a member of the interstellar community, before Viken was one planet among many.

The rebel faction leaders wanted war and strife, they each wanted to rule their own little kingdom with absolute control and iron fists. They wanted to believe they were omnipotent. Gods.

They were antiquated ideas leftover from thousands of years of culture. They had no place in the new world, in a world where the Hive could wipe out our entire planet's population in a matter of weeks if our foolish ways left them unprotected. We needed our warriors out in space, on the battleships, not bickering over backyard crops and women.

"You could have told us about the coalition's demands, about the warrior quotas falling," I said. "You could have told us about your plan, about our bride."

My brothers crossed their arms over their chests and nodded.

The old man arched one gray brow. "And would you have agreed? Would you have submitted to the matching process?" The regent tilted his head, the expression on his face one of relief. We were done arguing. He'd proven his point. I was not unreasonable, and neither, it would appear, were my brothers. We had not agreed, but we were listening.

Tor rubbed his jaw. "How did you match one of us? And to whom was this bride matched?"

The regent actually looked embarrassed, the pink in his cheeks a color I'd never before seen on his lined face. "The medical checkup you each had last month was a ruse for the testing. We sedated you and completed the testing while you were in a dream state. Some was done while you were completely unconscious."

At his words, I shuddered. I knew exactly what he spoke of. I'd gone in for a general health screening, as was required, and woken sweating, with my heart racing. The experience had been unusual. I'd never woken in a med unit with a hard cock before. Nothing I thought of had brought it down. I'd had to excuse the doctor and use my hand to alleviate the discomfort. It had been some kind of dream, something so intense that I'd been beyond aroused. The fuck if I remembered what I'd dreamed. "So, which one of us is her match?" I wanted to know. I needed to know. I did not want to fuck a female who wasn't mine. I'd do it once, if that was required to protect the planet, but I would not bond with her, I would not allow myself to care for her if she wasn't *mine*.

The regent chuckled. "All three of you. We combined your profiles in the program and she was matched to you, combined. She will not only accept all three of you, in the manner you each prefer, but she will *need* each of you to be truly happy. Each of you possesses a trait she needs, something she craves, something she will require to be made content." The regent paced, his hard gray boots peeking out from his robe as he walked. He wore a soft robe with battle-ready boots imbedded with blades. Soft words, followed by the sting of an iron will. The look suited him. "I did not wish to bring you here until the match had been made, until the transfer was to occur. I could not risk one of you refusing her."

Since that was blatant fact, none of us replied.

"Fine. Fine," Tor repeated. "So we are supposed to fuck this woman until we breed her? In the same room? At the same time?" he asked.

The regent shrugged. "You can share her, or you can take her one at a time. I'll leave the details to you."

Tor nodded. "Good. Then she will travel from sector to sector and we will each fuck her."

Regent Bard held up his hand. "As I said, you must each take her in a short time allotment to ensure that all of your seed merges and you all have an equal chance of siring. While fucking her together is not required to breed her, the mating laws do require—"

Lev ran his hand over the back of his neck and stood to pace. "Are you serious?"

Tor moved away from the wall. "We don't even like each

other and you expect us to come all over her at the same time?"

Anger flared at what the regent required. Taking turns was one thing, but together? We hadn't laid eyes on each other in thirty years and we were supposed to fuck her together?

The regent held up his hand again. "The law is clear. You know that a mating union must join all parties as one. In your case, with the three of you as her mates, you must all claim her at once. Otherwise, the bond is not sealed and she will be forever shunned."

Tor crossed his arms over his chest, his body rigid. Clearly, he didn't like that idea. "She will bear the child who unites the planet. How could she be shunned?"

"If you do not do this properly, your mate will be the vessel of the child's birth and nothing more. She will not be the ruling mother, or the mate of the sector leader. In her case, all three sector leaders. By law and custom, she will have been shunned by her mate. She will be banished."

I looked to my brothers, then at the regent. "We've been enemies our entire lives and you expect us to take her mouth, pussy, and ass at the same time for the mating union." I saw interest in my brothers' eyes, akin to how I felt. The idea was arousing, fucking a woman in any of those three ways, but I'd have to do it with men from sectors I'd been raised to dislike. Lev and Tor were my brothers by birth, but the people of Sector One were my people by blood and sweat and choice.

"For the mating union, yes. To breed her, no. You must each fill her pussy with seed, at least until she is properly bred. Once that is done, you may share her in any way you wish. But to do so, to ensure her happiness, you will need to put aside your differences."

All three of us arched our right brow and glared at the old man. Making sure our women were happy was a matter of pride with a warrior. To imply that we, the leaders of the planet, would be unable to satisfy all of our bride's needs was highly insulting. "You put us in different sectors to keep the peace, not to teach us tolerance. You kept us separated our entire lives and now you want us to pretend we are happy to fuck a woman together to ensure she is not shunned? To share a bride?"

"I agree with Drogan. A woman isn't going to solve our long-seated issues between sectors. Neither is a child."

"Well, sector leaders, I suggest you figure out how to unite the sectors, or all of Viken will fall to the Hive. You will lose everything. How precious your sector differences will be when you've all got so many neuro-processors implanted in your brains that you can't remember your own names." How the regent could remain calm was beyond me. I wanted to punch him in the nose for this alone. I wanted to pummel him for forcing all three of us to participate in this... insanity. For forcing our hands. For keeping the dangerous truth of our situation within the Interstellar Coalition a secret.

"Does our mate know she has been matched to three men?" Lev asked.

That was a good question and I looked to the regent.

"She does not. Her match was to your combined profile, just as each of you—" he pointed to each of us, "—were matched to hers. As triplets with identical DNA, she's matched to all three of you."

"Let me be clear, regent," Tor said. He used his fingers to tick off each of his items. "We have a mate who does not know that she belongs to three warriors. We have to convince her to fuck each of us. We must breed her immediately to unite the planet. And we must stabilize the sectors so that more warriors and brides are sent to the coalition or we will be overrun by the Hive."

"Yes. The coalition has given us ten months to improve our numbers."

That was barely enough time to breed our new bride and have a new little one crawling. The babe wouldn't be old enough to walk, and yet the child would be the acknowledged heir of all three planetary sectors.

I groaned. "We also have to convince our bride to accept our seed—at the same time—so the mating union is achieved. No mate of mine will be banished." Just breeding her was simple. We could fuck her any way we wished, but to achieve the mating union, we'd have to fuck her in all her holes at once. I wasn't a nice man, but I'd never see a woman shunned. Any issues I had about fucking her with my brothers were not her fault.

I didn't force a woman either. How we were going to persuade an unwilling woman to take on three men was not going to be easy. Perhaps facing the Hive would be easier.

"Nor mine," Lev grumbled.

Tor ticked off his last finger. "And we have to end thirty years of hatred and convince the planet to stand together."

When Tor explained all of that, it seemed an impossible task.

"How do we know she was not mated to another and you are using this as a way to manipulate us, to affect the balance of power between sectors?" I added.

At my question, my brothers pulled their shoulders back and loomed over the man.

"As you say, she would not have been sent here by her home world without being matched by the processing protocol." He sighed. "If it concerns you so greatly, I will summon other men to this room and she will be forced to choose you from among many."

"Only one of us," I said, ensuring that the woman made an impartial choice. If she were truly matched to one of us, the connection would be powerful and immediate. I'd forgotten that, so there was hope that she'd be inclined to our demands to fuck… immediately. I would not trust the match until our bride proved she was capable of feeling that connection.

The regent dipped his head respectfully. "Very well. As she believes she's only matched to one man, you will need to decide which of you will stand in the line. Remember, do what you must once you claim her. All three of you must coat her with your seed. Without the link and power of the seed power, the others will want her. They will try to take her from you."

Once a man's seed filled a woman's pussy, the bonding began. The chemicals in a Viken male's seed were powerful. Our bride would crave it, need it. In return, the man to whom she bonded would feel the constant urge to claim her, to protect her and renew the bond. That was the natural connection between a Viken man and his mate. But a few months without exposure to the bonding chemicals in a male's seed, and the woman's body would become receptive to the claim of another.

No woman of mine would ever suffer the loss of my seed bond. I would fuck her hard, and often. I would taste her pussy with my mouth as my seed filled her throat. I would—

"You think others will try to defy us by claiming our mate?" Lev asked. Until she chose one of us from the lineup, she was considered available. Any man powerful enough to take her from us could try to claim her.

"If she chooses one of us, then the match is true. She belongs to no one but us." Tor's words confirmed that he protected what was his. Lev nodded his agreement.

"The match is true. She will choose one of you," the regent said. He was very confident. Confident enough for me to believe he wasn't lying. If he were, this woman could choose any random Viken man in the room who would fuck her. He'd have seed power over her and the ability to breed her, not the three of us. His plan for one true leader would not occur.

"Surely this woman has been fucked before," Lev said. "Won't she be longing for the Earth man's cock she left behind? Won't she be suffering withdrawal of his seed?"

The regent shook his head. "Earth men do not have this connection with their mates. Their seed is not as potent as ours. This is in your favor. An Earth woman matched to three Viken men. Combined, your seed power will have a level of potency she can't imagine. Do your job, men, and do it well. Claim her, fuck her, fill her with your seed. Breed her. If, as you put it, you can't find unity between the three of you, go back to your sectors. Your mate will be banished once she gives birth. The child will rule. This petty feuding will end and we will take our rightful place as a fully protected member planet of the coalition once more. Nothing else matters."

The man had no sympathy for our individual desires. He was only thinking of the planet's stability. Not mine or my brothers' personal interests, and certainly not the wants or expectations of this woman we'd been matched to. Just like at our birth, we three brothers were casualties of circumstance once more. While Lev, Tor, and I could go back to our sectors if we did not agree to this shared mating, *she* would be ruined. Any child conceived would be ripped from her and from the mates who denied her. She would suffer for months from the strong, desperate pull of seed power from not just one man, but three.

It was not a fate I wished on any female, and particularly not one I was responsible for. Not one I had bred and claimed as my bride. A woman was to be protected and sheltered, pleasured and dominated. Not used, her trust gained, her obedience earned, only to be discarded by the mate she had been taught to serve. I glanced at my brothers. Could we overcome our differences to protect a female we had not met?

A bright light filled the room centering over the large table.

"Ah, her transport has begun." The regent looked giddy, a huge smile and expectant hop to his steps.

We all stepped back and watched as a woman slowly materialized on the table. Once the transport was complete, the blinding wash of light disappeared, leaving her unconscious form on the hard surface. We stepped closer to look at her, my eyes took a few seconds to adjust after the bright flash of her transport.

She wore a long dress typical on Viken. The material didn't hide her lush curves—very full breasts and curved hips. Her hair was dark red, the deepest color in a fire. It was unbound and lay in thick curls across the wood. Her lashes were long and rested against her pale cheeks. Her lips were a lush pink, plump and full and my cock pulsed at the idea of having them curved around it.

This was our mate? I glanced at my brothers whose expressions matched the awe I felt.

"You still feel it will be a hardship to fuck this woman? To be mated to her? To breed her?" The regent's words were intended to mock us, but instead highlighted the way each and every protest I had disappeared at the sight of her ripe body and beautiful face. I *wanted* her. I wanted my cock in her mouth and my hand striking her bare ass. I wanted to fuck her until she screamed and watch her kneel at my feet, naked and ready to be claimed.

No. Fucking her would be no hardship. My cock hardened at the sight of her, and she wasn't even conscious. Out of the corner of my eye, I saw Tor adjust himself. It was a good thing we were instantly drawn to her, for nothing less than the fate of the planet rested on our ability to fuck this woman and fuck her well.

• • • • • • •

Tor

We'd been called to the Viken United headquarters, not for a sector meeting, as I'd been told, but because my brothers and I were now forced by a threat to the planet to come together and breed a female assigned not just to me, but to my identical brothers as well. I knew I'd have to find a mate someday, but I had always believed it would be in my own time and a female of my own choosing. I'd also assumed my mate would be mine and mine alone. It seemed, as Regent Bard put it, fate intervened.

Here before me was the most beautiful female I'd ever seen, sprawled out on the table where the planet's boldest decisions were made. Perhaps *she* was one of the regents' boldest decisions. She would unite the sectors and bring supposed peace to the planet once again. She would inspire young warriors to war and virgin brides to offer themselves as mates. Her child would rule the planet when I and my brothers were long dead.

Separating my brothers and I had not united the planet. We were nothing but a temporary respite from all-out war. Our royal blood and our family's long history of fair and just rulers had calmed the planet enough for a tenuous peace to have taken hold. But separating us when we were mere infants had made us less than brothers. We had each been formed by the customs, biases, and beliefs of our specific sectors, nothing else. I was supposed to share this female with two men—brothers, even—I didn't know. We looked the same, but that was all. The regents expected us to share a mate. *Share!*

I had already been denied what should have been mine by right. In Sector One, where I ruled, family was all. Your worth was measured in the strength and honor of your family. I had none. My royal blood was all that had saved me from the life of an outcast among my own people. But even my blood had not been enough to save me from the taunts of cruel children, from the lonely reality of sitting alone at all major events. I was alone, always alone, and deemed vulnerable in a society where a familial shield ensured survival.

The isolation had made me strong, and I did not regret my life. But now, faced with creating a family of my own, I did not want to share my only family with two men I barely knew. I did not want to share the time or attentions of the female. If she was truly mine, as the regent claimed, I wanted her all to myself. I found that I was greedy for her love, her lust, her body. I wanted everything.

Looking at the lush curves of her ass and hips, I hardened at the idea of taking her in the ass, of stretching her and claiming her in all ways. Once I planted my child in her womb, I would then load her rounded ass with my seed, ensure her addiction to me, to my touch and to my cock. I wanted her to crave me entirely.

I wanted to scoop her up in my arms and carry this female to a quiet room and teach her how to fuck. I didn't doubt that my brothers would treat her well. Regardless of the political disagreements, all Viken men took care of their females and children. The women were protected and sheltered. A mate was cherished and valued as the most important thing in a man's life.

That, and that alone, was why I'd avoided a mate until now. I was not ready to make a female my everything. But now, now that I saw this… Earth female, things changed. I could see her heart thrumming against the long column of her neck. I could see the plump curves of her breasts above the neckline of her dress. I could imagine the silkiness of her red hair sliding through my fingers. Hell, I could even smell her. Something floral and clean. I wondered what she tasted like, if her pussy would be as sweet as the rest of her.

I adjusted my cock in my pants. There would be no relief until I was buried deep inside her.

"Do you still wish to have her choose you from a group?" the regent asked, his long gray robes billowing around his ankles as he turned to me.

I glanced at my brothers, who nodded. There was no denying the connection, but politics was ruthless. "Yes."

We had to ensure that this plan was valid, that the woman was truly ours. Testing the match would be the confirmation we needed, although I felt the pull by just looking at the female before us.

"Very well. I will organize the selection and return." Regent Bard nodded in my periphery, then walked from the room, the silent and forgotten Gyndar following.

"We don't even like each other. How are we going to do

this?" Drogan asked. He ran his hand through his slightly shorter hair in a gesture I recognized. I'd just done it a moment ago.

"Didn't they have triplet females on Viken that we could each have?" I leaned forward and placed my hands on the table. "It would solve the problem as easily as claiming one female," I added.

"The regents want one child, not three. One new leader," Lev clarified.

"Fuck," Drogan murmured.

The regent's plan was sound. He'd matched us to a female from another planet who could not return. Looking upon her, my cock stirred. I imagined my brothers' did as well. Once our seed was upon her, how could we deny the lust we would feel? She would be bound to us permanently, the scent of our seed in her system a siren's call to our senses. If we rejected her after she was bred, refusing the mating union, there was a very high probability she would go mad. We might not like each other, but we'd never hurt a woman. It would be better to kill her outright than to let her suffer with the call of three powerful Viken males' seed power unfulfilled.

Lev took a step closer to the table, studying our new mate. "How are we going to fuck her?"

Drogan and I moved closer until we all three stood over her, staring down with... awe. An argument was inevitable.

"I've heard men from Sector One like to fuck in public," Lev said, looking to me.

There was truth there. Fucking in my sector was not necessarily a private affair. Family ties were important. Sometimes, if a male wanted to breed his mate, and they wanted the child to be welcomed with open arms, he claimed her, impregnated her publicly. If a female suffered and needed her mate's seed, if the need was great enough, he took her whenever and wherever she needed him. A mate's needs came above all else.

I was accustomed to being watched, to watching others,

so if I had to witness my brothers fucking, it would not be a hardship. What would be difficult was to watch them fuck *her*.

"Sector Two men need to tie a mate down in order to get her beneath him," I countered.

Lev's jaw clenched. "We do not bind our women to rape them. There is pleasure in the taking, and the women eagerly submit."

"She is bound. She has no choice," Drogan added.

Lev looked ready to kill. "She *wants* to be bound, to submit." He turned to Drogan. "Why are you so bothered by what we do in Sector Two? Sector Three men eat pussy like it's candy. I've heard you prefer eating pussy to actually fucking."

Drogan grinned, not bothered at all by Lev's statement. "We do enjoy a nice wet female, sometimes for hours." Drogan's eyes darkened with the same lust I was feeling as he stared at our new mate. "I can't wait to get my mouth between her thighs and taste her. To use my tongue over her little clit ring and bring her to orgasm again and again. To hear her beg." He leaned over and inhaled deeply, drawing her scent into his lungs. "I will taste her until she screams, and then I will fuck her until she screams for more."

Our bickering stopped as we all seemed to be lost in our personal fantasies. It was obvious to me that we all had an identical reaction to the female. I looked, and I lusted. I wanted to throw her over my shoulder and take her home, strap her down in the town square, and fuck her with the entire town watching me plant my seed in her womb.

But that wouldn't happen now. We would have to claim her here, at Viken United. Here, on this island of neutral ground. And it would have to be done with my brothers.

She hadn't moved and we stood staring at her as if she were a puzzle we could not solve.

"We can agree that fucking her will not be a chore," Lev said. "However we go about it, however it makes our cocks hard, it will be a pleasure."

"Yes," I agreed. My cock was already hard and I was just looking at her completely clothed. I could only imagine how I'd feel once she was naked before us.

"Yes," Drogan confirmed.

"Can we agree then—" I began, shifting my cock in my pants, "—that we should focus not on our differences, but focus on what we now must protect and cherish together. *Her.*"

"If he expects us to breed her and then abandon her and the child, he is mistaken," I said, my voice laced with the lifetime of anger. "Sector One's belief in family—a mother and a father caring for their children—is very specific. I won't let this child grow up as I have." I offered each of my brothers a quick glance. "I will kill anyone who tries to take her, or my child, from me."

I'd been an orphan. No real mother or father. I'd been raised by the government, by nannies and tutors, without a family. It had not been easy. In fact, it had been fucking awful. There was no way I'd subject anyone to that, let alone my very own child.

"The politics behind this can wait. Once she awakens, she cannot," Lev replied.

"Neither can my cock," Drogan muttered.

Both Lev and I smiled at that.

We looked down upon her for a moment. "She will be afraid. She belongs to not one man, but three," Drogan said. "Look at us."

I glanced at my brothers. We were big and troublesome, cranky and aggressive. We were bred to be leaders; our size, our power, made us fierce. "We are not tame," I added.

"We may not have like minds on much, but we must agree about her and how we take her." Lev angled his head at the sleeping woman. "I refuse to let her suffer. As Tor said, I refuse to leave a child to grow up under the regent's care."

He spat the word "care," for the regent wouldn't care

for a child any more than he would a family pet.

Drogan nodded and looked at me and Lev. "She is ours."

"If this isn't a trap and she chooses us," I confirmed. "Agreed?"

"Agreed," Lev and Drogan replied at the same time.

"Which one of us will stand with the other men to prove the match?" Drogan asked.

"Doesn't matter," I replied. "She'll choose one of us from the group. The regent wouldn't go through all of this if he wasn't sure of the match."

"This is for our benefit. I agree with Tor," Lev commented. "It matters not who stands with the others as long as we take her away from here together. No one else touches her."

"Agreed."

CHAPTER THREE

Leah

My eyes blinked open as if I'd just taken a nap. Just seeing a ceiling made of dark paneled wood was enough to nudge my brain into realizing that I was no longer in the processing center. It was quiet, no hum of the air conditioning, no machines. The air was warm and humid. A rustle had me turning my head. I seemed to be resting on a hard table and an old man sat in a high-backed chair at its edge. Using my hand on the wood, I pushed myself up to sitting. I wore a green dress, simple in design, yet long. It covered my legs to my ankles, yet my feet were bare. It had long sleeves but a low-cut bodice. It wasn't overly revealing, but I was fairly large so I always had cleavage. The dress was odd, old-fashioned in style, something a woman would have worn a hundred years earlier.

The man sat so still, so patiently. He had gray hair and a beard, the deep grooves of old age lined his face. His attire was similar to mine, simple and unadorned, but gray. "Are you… are you the man who is my match?" I asked. I cleared my throat, my voice sounding scratchy. Had they sent me to such an old man? He had to be eighty, if he was a day.

He smiled then, the creases at the corners of his eyes becoming deeper. "I am not. I am Regent Bard. Your match is just out that door." I looked in the direction he pointed. "When you are ready, we can go to him."

"I am on Viken, right?" The room was large, yet sparse. The floor was of similar wood to the ceiling, the walls white. There were windows on the long ends of the room, but the only thing I could see beyond them was greenery. I didn't feel like I was off-planet, or that I'd traveled halfway across the galaxy. I felt like I was in an ancient building looking out at an old growth forest near the sea. I could smell damp and salt, heavy and thick, saturating the air as only a large body of water could.

It wasn't like the sci-fi movies on TV. He didn't wear silver. He didn't have a third arm. He didn't even look the least bit green. He looked normal. Old, but normal.

"Yes. Welcome to Viken, my lady. What is your name?"

"Leah." I didn't mean to be rude, but my match was nearby. I just had to tell this man I was ready and he would take me to him. Was I ready? Would I ever be? The good news was that I wasn't on Earth. My fiancé couldn't reach me here and no one could send me back.

However, the *idea* of going off-planet and being fucked and claimed by a complete stranger had *seemed* sound, but the *reality*, actually being here was a little scary. I knew nothing about the planet Viken or what Vikens looked like. What did my match look like? I'd never even considered the possibility of his age or his appearance. I hadn't wanted a mate, not really. I'd simply wanted to escape the vile man who wanted to treat me like chattel on Earth. But now, now I was... nervous.

Regardless, I was here on another planet and I couldn't escape my destiny. So I took a deep breath and said, "I'm ready."

He stood slowly and held out a hand, helping me down from the table. My long dress fell to my ankles, the material heavy. I followed him to the door. As I walked, I felt a slight tugging on my clit. Odd. I paused mid-step at the zing that coursed through me, shrugged it off. When I took another two steps and I felt it again, I knew something wasn't right.

I blushed, for I couldn't tell this old man that there was something wrong with my clit, nor could I pull up the long length of my dress to investigate, no matter how curious I was. Heat washed over me, not from embarrassment, but from newfound desire, and I licked my lips. I wanted to reach down and touch myself, but that wasn't appropriate. Was this new sensation because I was on Viken? I had to worry about it later, so I bit down on my lip and passed through the door he held open.

The connecting room was equally large, but with no table. Only a few chairs lined the walls. The room wasn't my focus, but the men lined up before me. They were all tall and muscular, quite large. In fact, *very* large. It seemed Viken men appeared to be almost exactly like Earth men, but impressively bigger. All of them stared at me with interest and curiosity. I had to remember that they probably hadn't seen a woman from Earth before. We were equally intrigued.

The old man now stood beside me and lifted his chin in the direction of the line of men. "Your match was successful; however, on Viken, proof of the connection is required."

I turned my head and looked down at him. "Connection?"

"A natural bond between a matched pair." When I continued to frown, he explained. "Just walk past all of the men and tell me which one is your match."

"Just… just walk past them and I'll know?" I glanced at the men. They gave nothing away, only avid curiosity. There were at least ten men in all, all in their prime. Some were more handsome than others, some stared at me like I was a curiosity and some like they wanted to devour me where I stood. One man in particular watched me as if he could see the flutter of my pulse racing in my neck, as if he counted the rapid rise and fall of my panicked breathing. I met his gaze and quickly looked away, frightened and feeling like a fawn being stalked by a panther.

The men all wore similar clothing and it seemed there were two kinds of warriors: barbarians in furs and leathers and scholars in robes. Both types of men carried weapons strapped to their backs: swords, bows, and spears. For an advanced race, an alien race, they appeared to be rather primitive in the ways they made war.

I felt like I'd stepped off Earth and into an episode of my favorite Viking television show. If the men had grown beards, they would have looked like medieval warriors from ancient Earth.

How would I know which of these men was mine? What if I chose the wrong man by mistake? "Is this a trick? Are you planning to send me back to Earth if I choose the wrong warrior?"

Panic flared at the idea of ending up back on Earth. Warden Egara would shake her head in disgust and I'd be kicked out of the processing center. I'd be alone, penniless and lost, and I had no doubt that my fiancé would find me and punish me for running away. Perhaps this time he would not stay his hand. Perhaps he would just strangle me and be done with it.

"I am not trying to deceive you." The older gentleman's words startled me from my musings as he gave a casual shrug. "As to knowing your match, you will have no doubt. His body and his soul will call to yours. Do not be afraid. Trust in your match."

I didn't seem to have much of a choice. I started at the left side of the line, moved to stand before the first man and gave him a timid smile. I ignored my tingling clit. It had nothing to do with this man, and I wondered if the transport here had somehow put my body off kilter.

Focus. I had to focus on the task at hand. The first man had blond hair, similar age to me, rugged-looking despite the bow strapped to his back and the long black robe covering his body. He smiled at me, his eyes alight with male interest, but I felt nothing unusual. I moved on to the second man. He was slightly shorter, but heavier and more muscular. He had long hair as pale as snow and was wearing the more primitive leather and furs. A sword was slung over his back, reminding me of a Viking invader of old. He did not smile at me. He did not even look me in the eye. He undressed me with his eyes, his gaze focused on the hard nipples clearly visible beneath my soft green gown. I gave him the same cursory glance and still… nothing. I worked my way down the line until there were only a few men to go, worried that none of the men were my match. Was this a trick? Would the regent be disappointed or upset if I didn't recognize the match?

I stepped before the next man and looked up at him nervously. This was the man who had watched me earlier, who had studied me from across the room as if I already belonged to him. I halted, turning to face him and looked up. Way up. He was taller than the others, broader across the shoulders. He was rugged, wearing the Viking-style clothing and a sword across his back. His chest and arms were massive, his hands looked large enough that one of them could completely wrap around my neck. His thighs were thick as tree trunks and he exuded strength and authority.

But it wasn't his physique that had my heart skipping a beat, but the look in his dark eyes. They didn't just look at me, but stared into me, into my soul. My nipples tightened and my pussy clenched at the very sight of him. I gasped at my body's reaction as wet heat flooded my pussy. His nostrils flared and his jaw clenched. I could even pick up his clean scent, spicy and woodsy. Was he smelling me, too?

I didn't realize the regent had come to stand beside me until he spoke. "I assume you do not need to look over the remaining two men?" he asked.

I hadn't taken my eyes off of the man before me. His hair was tousled, as if he'd just climbed out of bed, and just long enough to graze the collar of his dark tunic. The color of it was an unusual shade of brown, almost whiskey-colored. I knew, deep down, that he was the one. He was my match.

I swallowed down my eagerness for this man and replied, "No, I do not. This man is my match."

"Satisfied, Drogan?" the regent asked.

This warrior, Drogan, lowered his gaze from my eyes to rake over my body. I felt naked despite being covered to my ankles by the long green gown. Did he know I was aroused at the sight of him? Did he know my body ached when I looked at him, that as much as I feared him, I craved the touch of those giant hands on my skin? Whatever was going on with my clit intensified and I shifted uncomfortably on my feet. Waiting. For what I wasn't sure.

"Yes. Very satisfied." Drogan's deep voice invaded my senses like liquid heat overrunning my entire system. I wanted to hear his voice again, to hear him commanding me to kneel and take his cock in my mouth, to listen to him order me to open wider as he pounded into my body, to hear the gravelly whisper of his voice in my ear demanding that I come.

I blinked away the lust clouding my mind, but didn't even have a chance to recover before my world upended. Drogan tossed me over his shoulder as if I were a sack of grain and carried me out of the room. My hands pressed into his lower back to maintain my balance and all I could see was the tight muscles of his very nice ass as he carried me out of the building, down a dirt path, and toward another much smaller building a good distance away.

All around me the smell of sea water and blooming trees comforted me. The sky was a bit darker blue, the grass a paler green, and the sounds of the birds and other animals calling to one another not any that I recognized, but it was not so different from Earth after all. I saw red flowers, trees hung with dark green moss and long pale limbs that stretched toward the sky.

Here, on Viken, I would be safe from my old fiancé. Here, I would be protected and claimed by this man, Drogan. He was huge and fierce-looking, but I wanted to trust in the match. I wanted to believe Warden Egara and what she told me, that this man had been selected for me, was my one perfect man in the entire universe. I had to hope that I could grow to love him, and he to care for me. Being tossed over his shoulder and carried about in such a caveman way wasn't the way to show how much he cared, but it definitely made me feel wanted.

I watched as his foot kicked the door shut behind him right before he slid me carefully down his body to stand before him. I swear I felt every hard inch of him on the way down.

I looked up at him again as I held onto his forearms for balance. I could barely breathe, my longing to taste him was so intense. I studied his lips as he spoke, hoping he would lean down and claim my mouth with his own, needing to feel like I belonged to him. Only to him.

"I am Drogan, your match." Slowly, with his hands on my shoulders, he turned me around to face…

"Oh, my God," I whispered, my eyes widening.

"These are my brothers. They belong to you as well." Before me stood two more men, identical to Drogan. Triplets? Holy shit. No. Not three—

"I am Tor. Your match."

"I am Lev. Your match."

I spun to the side so I could see all three of them, my head turning back and forth as if I were watching a tennis match. Tor had long hair. Lev, short. Drogan in the middle. They were all dressed like Viking warriors: Lev with a bow and arrows across his back, Tor with a spear and shield, and Drogan with a sword. I felt like I was Little Red Riding Hood with three wolves who all wanted to eat me alive. While I was completely confused and overwhelmed, I felt the connection become even stronger.

"Identical triplets?" I squeaked. I'd never seen identical

triplets. Handsome, *male* identical triplets. Seeing three such gorgeous men was akin to seeing a unicorn. These three were matched to me. Of all the people in the universe, these hot guys were mine to choose from. Three. I didn't want three men. Just one. I only needed one.

They nodded in response to my question.

"There are slight differences between us. I have a scar," Lev said as he pointed to his eyebrow. A white line bisected his eyebrow.

"I have a sector marking." Tor rolled up the sleeve of his shirt to show me the dark band that circled his arm. A tattoo. It looked like something tribal from Earth.

"I do not have any distinguishing feature, but our hair length should help you tell us apart," Drogan added.

"I can't... be matched to all *three* of you." But I was. I knew deep down that I was because I felt the same attraction, the same pull with all three of them. It wasn't just with Drogan; the longing I felt to be touched by Drogan was now an ache to be touched by all three men. Lev and Tor's pull on me was equally strong, and terrifying. "Which one of you gets me?"

"We have the same DNA. While three different men, we are biologically the same," Lev explained.

"So which one of you is my match?" Perhaps this was some kind of test. Perhaps they would decide now which one was my mate and the others would go home.

They stepped closer.

"Gets you?" Lev asked, arching his scarred eyebrow.

"The one who keeps me. Did you decide or do I choose one of you, or what?"

They moved in so they all stood directly before me, towering over me as the top of my head barely reached their chins. If I lifted my hand, I could reach out and touch them. Their bodies shadowed the light from the windows and I felt very, *very* small.

"We decided," Tor said and my shoulders sagged with relief. I could not choose. I could not. The pull I felt for each of them was simply too strong. Better to let them choose and simply accept whichever brother claimed me.

"We're all keeping you."

I took a step back. Had I heard them correctly? All three—

"You can't all… I mean surely…" I couldn't get the words out. I didn't understand. It made no sense that they would all want me. On Earth this would never be allowed; the morality council would arrest me for even thinking such lascivious thoughts. "I can't be with all three of you. It's not done. It's *illegal*," I whispered.

Lev shook his head. "There is no law that says a woman cannot be shared. Besides, we've been matched to you. The match is legally binding in itself."

"I could request another," I said quickly.

They descended upon me again and I retreated until my back bumped into the wall. "You won't." Drogan's dark eyes locked with mine and my heart pounded so hard I feared it would leap from behind my ribcage onto the floor.

How dare they be so big and bossy! "Oh?" I crossed my arms over my chest. "And why is that?"

"Because unlike most females through the bride program, you have *three* men who are matched to you. Three. The connection is very powerful with just one mate. With three, I imagine it is almost keen."

He enunciated the last as their hands lifted and they touched me. Tor's hand stroked over my hair, Lev and Drogan touched my shoulders and slid their hands down my arms. *Keen* wasn't the word for it. It was razor sharp, intense, hot, searing. Oh, hell, I had no idea what it was. I just knew I'd never felt it before and I… I liked it.

My eyes slipped closed at the warm feel of their hands on me. They weren't touching me inappropriately, just… touching. The forbidden desire that gripped me made me clench my teeth. Would they bind me to a special bench as I'd seen during my processing? Would they fill my pussy and my ass at the same time? Would two suckle at my breasts while the third fucked me? Would I let them? My mind said no, but my pussy clenched at the idea of being shared by them and I pressed my thighs together in an attempt to stop the ache.

"Tell us your name."

With my eyes closed, I didn't know who spoke. "Leah," I whispered.

"Leah, we are going to fuck you now," a man said. It wasn't a question. He wasn't asking, he was telling.

I opened my eyes and stared at them, one, then the next, then the next. "No dinner? No movie? Not even foreplay?"

They stared at me curiously. "We are not aware of what a movie is, but if you are hungry, we will certainly see to your needs." Lev meant his words sincerely, but I couldn't help but laugh.

"I don't even know you and you just expect me to fuck all three of you?"

Tor tucked my hair behind my ear, then dipped down so he was at my eye level. "I sense you are nervous."

My eyes widened. "You think?"

"Have you ever been fucked before? Are you a virgin?"

I hadn't been a virgin since the night of high school graduation. That was *not* the problem. "I am not a virgin."

"You do not long for the man who first claimed you, who filled you with his seed?"

"Long for him?" Did I long for Seth Marks who took my virginity in his parents' basement? He'd fumbled putting the condom on and the whole uninspiring event had been over in about thirty seconds. I hadn't even gotten over the pain of it all before he was finished. I did *not* long for him.

"Um… no. No seed filling." I heard he had moved to Arizona and was now a tennis pro at some resort.

All three men actually relaxed, which surprised me. The testing process had confirmed, not once, but twice, that I was unmarried. Warden Egara knew I was eager to leave Earth. I had no strings, no love affairs worth remembering, certainly not a kid from high school who didn't know what a clit was. I'd had bigger problems to worry about with a dangerous and obsessive fiancé.

Drogan tugged his shirt from his pants and lifted it over his head, then dropped it on the floor behind him.

"What are you doing?" I squeaked, my eyes glued to his chiseled body. Holy hell, I was matched to *that*?

"Making you more comfortable," he replied.

"How is taking off your shirt making me more comfortable?" It was making me a tad nervous and very hot. I wanted to reach up and touch him, to feel the warmth of his skin, the softness of the springy hairs on his chest, the ridges of his abs. He was very hard to resist.

"Would you rather us take off your dress?"

All three men looked very eager to do so. The fact that they were giving me a choice, or at least pretending to do so, made this a little easier.

"Oh… um, probably not."

Drogan glanced at his brothers and they stepped back and started shedding their clothes. Piece by piece more and more of their identical, very hot bodies appeared. I gulped at the sight of them. What these men did on Viken, I had no idea. It was not sitting in an office or pushing papers around.

It was when they lowered their pants—no underwear underneath—and stood tall before me, naked, that I stared. I didn't breathe. I couldn't believe what I was seeing. Perhaps I stared too long because they glanced down at themselves. "Are we not formed like men on Earth?"

They were *not* formed like men on Earth, or any man on Earth I'd ever seen… between their legs. Their cocks were huge, like swollen, pulsing clubs extending from their bodies. Dark veins bulged along their lengths, very thick, the flared crowns nearly reached their navels yet pulsed toward me. That was stunning enough, but what had me ogling them was that their cocks were all pierced. I knew that some men on Earth had their cocks pierced with a ring, similar to a large hoop earring, but I'd never seen one before. The metal on my mates' cocks shined like polished silver and circled from the small hole at the center of the crown to disappear underneath.

I knew that different piercing styles had names, but for the life of me, I had no idea what it was called. It was carnal. Wicked. Erotic.

Drogan gripped his cock at the base and began stroking up the long length. Fluid seeped from the tip and dripped from the metal ring.

"Um…." I was at a complete loss for words at the sight. "Earth men are the same, but smaller."

All three men glanced down, taking in their cocks. Since they were identical, it wasn't as if they had to compare. They were all huge. If they were on Earth, they could easily become very famous, very rich porn stars. I stifled a laugh, thinking how I had been matched to three identical, gorgeous, well hung, interstellar porn stars.

"Smaller? Earth men's cocks are smaller? Pity for Earth women." Lev looked at me and winked. "Lucky for you. You're going to like fucking us much better."

Us.

"I've never seen rings *there* before."

Tor began stroking his cock as well. "Men on Earth don't have their cocks pierced?"

"Some, perhaps, but it's not usual."

"It's usual here. It's a rite of passage to being a man."

"Trust me, you're going to love it." Lev stepped up to me and stroked my cheek with his knuckles. Having to tilt my head back helped keep me from staring at his cock, but I could feel it pressing, hard and thick, against my belly, the ring at first cool, then growing warmer.

"We must fuck you, Leah. Now."

"Because you're horny?" I asked. Seriously, no foreplay at all?

"Because it's not safe for you here unless you're marked by our seed."

I was about to laugh at the ridiculousness of that

statement, but the three men did not seem to be in a joking mood. Still, I had to ask. "Seriously?"

It was Lev's turn to frown. "Your safety is crucial."

"You three are naked and stroking your cocks and talking about my safety. I have a hard time seeing how it's tied to your *seed*." I held up my hand. "If you're trying to get me into bed, this isn't the way to do it."

Drogan and Tor didn't stop stroking themselves, but decided to have a conversation while doing so.

"The regent said Earth men have no seed power."

"Then she might not recognize the reason behind our urgency."

Lev kept his eyes on me, but added, "There is much to tell you." He took my hand. "Come." He led me across the room to a bed I hadn't noticed before. It could have been because I'd been over Drogan's shoulder when I'd come in. The style of the house—was that what it was called?—was similar to the other building I had arrived in. Wood floors, similar wood ceiling, white walls, square windows, and minimal furnishing. Based on the clothes and the appearance of the buildings, this was not a high-tech planet.

I stood before the bed, staring at where the men were going to take me. Not one, not two, but three!

"I will tell you some things about Viken." Lev stood behind me and placed his hot hands on my shoulders, his heat sinking into my body through the thin gown I wore.

"Be quick about it," Drogan said, his voice deeper and his cock… had it gotten even bigger?

Lev leaned over and whispered in my ear, his hot breath making me shiver. "Viken men all have rings in their cocks. Trust me, you will like it very much. As for our seed, it is potent. Once it touches your skin, but most especially fills your pussy, our bonding will begin. Other men will know you belong to us and it will prevent you from seeking the cock of another."

"I seem to have three men. Why would I need another cock?"

Tor smiled on my left, his hand wrapped around the head of his cock and his eyes glued to my breasts. "Indeed."

Lev leaned in, pressing his cock to my ass. I froze as his hands landed on the flare of my hips before exploring the curve of my waist and coming up to cup my breasts. I gasped and squirmed, not ready for this, for them, but as gentle as his hands were on my body his arms were like steel beams holding me in place for his exploration. "If you leave this dwelling without our seed in you, on you, marking you with our claim and our scent, you can fall prey to any man who wishes to claim you. Do you wish to be with all three of your matches? Or would you prefer a stranger?"

It was difficult enough keeping up with the men I was matched with. I couldn't think it would be any easier with a man who did not have any connection with me. And when I saw Drogan in the line of men, I definitely *felt* the connection. I felt it even more now, with Lev pressed to my back and the other two watching like hunters waiting to strike.

"I don't want anyone else."

"Then it is time for us to fuck you."

"But… you can't just expect me to lay back and spread my legs?" I pointed to the bed. "It doesn't work that way for me."

"Leah," Drogan said, his thumb swiping over more pre-cum that slid from the tip of his cock. "It doesn't work that way for us either."

"That's… that's good to hear." I was flustered and nervous and glad they weren't rutting beasts, although if I had a little foreplay first, that might not be so bad. "I'm the one that's going to have to take on three men."

Tor came up to face me and swept my hair to the side, his hands resting gently on my shoulders, his thumbs stroking my neck. "With your pussy, mouth, and ass all filled at once?"

I shuddered at the images that invaded my mind. I wasn't ready for that, but my body definitely liked the idea.

"We will not take you like that... today, at least."

As he kissed the side of my neck, Lev began to undo buttons down my back. I couldn't see them, but I knew what it felt like for them to be tugged open one at a time.

"I'm... I'm scared," I admitted, biting my lip.

"Three men would be daunting, especially three Viken men." Lev crooned from behind me.

"You've just arrived here and must be fucked right away. We do not doubt your feelings, but you should not be fearful of us. We will only bring you pleasure." Tor kissed my neck once again, the heat of his mouth gentle and yet very arousing. It was a simple gesture and I liked it much more than being tossed on the bed and forced.

"We would never hurt you. We will never let *anyone* hurt you," Lev vowed.

The others murmured their agreement.

"I can see you are aroused by us," Tor commented.

I frowned. "You can?" My pussy *was* damp, but surely they couldn't know that.

"Your cheeks are flushed," Lev said. "Your nipples are hard."

I looked down at myself and sure enough, my nipples stood out against the fabric of my dress, so I crossed my arms over them. Of course, that only made my cleavage practically bulge out the top.

"Is this dress normal for Viken?" I felt like I stepped out of an Old West movie, except these men were definitely not cowboys.

"Yes," Drogan said. "While a woman should be modest in front of others, a female is expected to be anything but with her mate."

"Mates," Tor clarified.

"I am... aroused by you." I looked at each of them as I admitted this. "It's not normal though, to just fuck three strangers."

They glanced at each other. "I sense your continued reticence and we wish to make it easier for you. I will cover your eyes." Drogan held a long strip of cloth up and I bit my lip. "While all three of us will be here, touching you, pleasuring you, you will not know whose mouth is on your pussy, whose hands are cupping your breasts, whose cock is deep inside you. Perhaps not seeing the three of us tend to you will be easier to accept."

CHAPTER FOUR

Leah

Blindfolded? Was he trying to be kinky? The idea of not being able to see and being at the men's mercy didn't make me panic. It made my pussy clench. I was naked beneath the gown; I could feel the smooth glide of the fabric on my bare ass. Ever since I arrived on Viken I had felt a twinge of lust centered around my clit and I definitely didn't feel like I had anything on beneath this gown. Lev could lift it right now and take me from behind. Or lift me as Tor fucked me in the air.

God, what was wrong with me? I wanted them to do it all. I wanted them to make me scream. I needed to feel owned and pleasured, and totally and completely claimed. Only then would I feel safe here, only then would I stop fearing a return trip to Earth.

"All… all right."

I wasn't on Earth anymore. I did not have to live by Earth's rules. I had three identical hot men who wanted to fuck me. Why should I deny them? It wasn't as if they planned to fuck me and leave me. They were mine just as I was theirs. I was their match.

My girlfriends—the ones I had before I became engaged—

Drogan lifted the piece of fabric up to cover my eyes as Tor slid down to kneel before me, his hands resting possessively on the curve of my hips. Lev took the ends of the blindfold and tied the soft fabric behind my head as Drogan's hands settled over my large breasts. Lev kissed the back of my neck, carefully tucking my hair out of the way. I was surrounded by them, and giving them control. I wouldn't even be able to see which one of them stroked me, or whose cock filled my pussy.

"No one... no one else will come in?"

"No one," Drogan murmured, then kissed the side of my neck. "We will share you between us, but with no one else."

As the world went dark my other senses instantly increased. I licked my lips, nervous. I could hear their breathing. I noticed their scent. Something woodsy and dark. When Lev's hands finished opening the buttons down the back of my dress, it slipped off my shoulders and fell like silk unveiling a statue. The fabric slid softly over my breasts and hips to pool on the floor at my feet. The air caressed my bare skin.

"We will move now, so that you do not know who it is that touches you."

They left me standing alone for several seconds, pacing across the room and coming back to me one by one. I did not know whose hands went to my breasts. I gasped as I was kneaded and caressed, thumbs brushing over my hard and aching nipples.

Another set of hands slid over my belly, my hips, then down the outside of my legs. One hand hooked my knee and I was forced to step wider. That same hand worked its way up the inside of my thigh to my pussy. He wasn't quick about it, but he didn't linger either.

"So pink."

"Pretty nipples."

"Full pussy lips."

I couldn't tell who was talking, for their voices were the same, but I shifted uncomfortably under their scrutiny.

"I will mark her now." I could hear the sound of one of them stroking his cock. It was distinctive even over the thrumming of my heart.

"Guys, I'm not sure—"

"And this. She is adorned beautifully. So smooth. So soft."

Someone touched my clit and my hips jerked at the intensity of it. It was sharp and bright and powerfully arousing. "Oh, God, what… what was *that*?"

"You do not have clit rings on Earth?"

I stilled for a moment as I processed what he said, and the feeling of soft lips on my body. A clit ring? A finger slid over my pussy.

"I have no hair," I said, more to myself than to the three men as a finger slid over me unhindered. I was completely bare. While I had shaved and kept my pussy trimmed neatly, this was something else entirely.

The mate kneeling before me pressed me with fingers and lips and the heated glide of his tongue. "Your pussy lips are smooth beneath my fingers and very pale. You are pink, and swollen, and glistening with sweet nectar." But I struggled to focus on his words because it wasn't his words that held my focus, it was the pull of his kiss on my new clit ring. I had not seen the ring, but I knew of them. I imagined his tongue circling and sucking at the tiny circle of metal that had been inserted into the hood. He flicked his tongue over it gently and a pulse of pleasure spread from there to my core, to tighten my nipples and make me gasp. It was very sensitive.

"I'm not going to last watching her like this," one of them said as he continued to stroke himself. I could hear the meaty glide of his fist over his cock, the recognizable sound of a man pleasuring himself. His hand began to move faster and he stepped closer.

"I've never... I mean, a ring, why?"

The one kneeling before me continued to play with the clit ring with his tongue as his hands moved to the insides of my knees, pushing them wider so he could gain better access, could stroke me with the full length of his tongue. Could fuck me with the exploratory tip and suck.

My knees buckled and strong arms caught me from behind as the sensual assault continued on both at my breasts and on my core. The man at my back pressed his hard cock to my ass, his thick voice filling my ear. "All mated women are adorned this way. It makes fucking much more pleasurable. More important, there will be no question, by any male, that you belong to us."

"Touch me," the voice behind me growled. Unable to resist his command, I reached behind me and wrapped my small hand around his very thick and swollen shaft. Fluid seeped from the tip and down over my fingers. It was hot and slick and it felt incredible as it touched my skin. "Harder, mate. Make me come."

I did as he bid, for I couldn't help myself.

Would I always feel the clit ring as I walked? Would it always make me aroused?

"Squeeze me hard. Do it now," he growled.

I felt his cock buck and jerk in my hand as thick ropes of cum shot from his engorged shaft, landing on my ass and the curve of my lower back. It was warm against my skin. Pulse after pulse, it landed on me. He exhaled once he was spent and the three men froze around me as if waiting for my reaction. I'd never before had my body marked by the wet crisscrosses of cum.

I let go of his cock and while he'd just released his essence, it was still hard. As I released him his hands shifted from my waist to smear his cum over my ass like lotion. "Can you feel it?" he whispered.

I frowned, thinking his actions odd. Most men would get a cloth and wipe the seed from me, but he coated my ass with it, even slid down and ran his slick fingers over my folds, mingling our fluids.

Wherever he touched I felt a warm glow, as if he were spreading a medicinal cream designed to heat my skin. Between my legs, it was even hotter, making my clit pulse and ache. My attention centered on his large, blunt fingers—glistening with his seed—gently moving between my legs and over my ass.

The man before me sucked hard on my clit, the other lowered his hot mouth to my nipple with a soft bite and my knees turned to jelly. I *could* feel something moving through my system now like the rush of a drug thundering through my bloodstream. But I wasn't drugged, I was aroused. Needy. Empty.

"I'm going to fall."

In one quick motion, the mate behind me lifted me in his arms—not over his shoulder this time—and carried me to the bed, laying me gently upon it. The blanket was cool beneath my heated skin. Something was happening to me. When I'd been with a man in the past, it had taken time, and plenty of foreplay to be aroused enough for sex, and even then, I'd had to touch myself to come. I'd only had two lovers before, but neither could get me off on his own. I always had to help.

But lying here blindfolded, I could feel the hot pull of three warriors looming over me. I felt small, helpless, and completely at their mercy. I imagined them with identical dark looks on their faces, lust and hunger and unforgiving demand. Lying here, I was closer to coming than I ever had been with another man—and they'd barely touched me.

"The seed is working," one of them commented. Reaching forward, he grabbed my ankles and tugged me down the bed so that I was settled at the very edge. Dropping to his knees, he spread my thighs wide, placing one leg, then the other, over his shoulders.

"Men from Sector Three love to eat pussy." His thumbs stroked over my swollen folds. "I am no exception, mate. This pussy is mine."

He lowered his head and ran his tongue up the length of my seam, then finished by flicking the ring with his tongue.

I dropped back onto the bed with a soft moan as a broad tongue invaded my pussy in a hard, quick thrust. The blindfold remained over my eyes and as my mate's mouth worked my core, another leaned in close and whispered his promise against my lips. "We're going to fuck you, Leah. All three of us. But not until you come for us."

"But—"

The intensity of the pleasure of the tongue on my clit was too much. When he slipped a finger inside of me, I clenched down, eager for something to fill me. But it was when his lips locked over my clit sucking hard and he curled the fingers inside me to stroke my G-spot—God, yes! I had one—that my hips bucked and I cried out. Loudly.

What was happening to me? I'd just met these men and I was naked, legs spread wide with one of them licking and nibbling at my pussy. Three men! I was a slut. Something happened in transport and I was now a total, wanton slut. But the way my mate so skillfully brought me closer and closer to coming with his mouth, I couldn't convince myself to care.

"It's so good," I moaned.

"Only good?" I heard. "Let's make it better than that."

The voice sounded as if I'd insulted them. A large hand wound into my hair, twisting and pulling until my head arched back with a slight whisper of pain. Instead of protesting, I arched my breasts into the air with a soft cry. I wanted more. I needed more. As if they could read my mind, a second hand landed to cover my throat and gently squeezed, not a threat, but ownership, a demand for trust.

I should have been afraid, I should have begged them to stop, but their touch made me wild, beyond thought. With one mate's mouth and fingers stroking my core, I lost all sense of myself as a hot mouth latched onto each of my nipples, sucking and tugging on them. They held me down, and I could not see, could not protest. I could do nothing but shatter.

I came. I screamed. I thrashed. I soared.

It was like an out of body experience, the pleasure so incredible it was bright and hot and blinding, even with my eyes covered. The men didn't relent, didn't give me a second to recover, for their mouths didn't stop, and the thick and wickedly talented fingers continued to slide deep inside me.

Sweat broke out on my skin. My heart was pounding in my chest. I couldn't catch my breath as they took me over again.

As I lay limp and replete, my legs were lifted off my mate's shoulders. Large hands pushed my knees back toward my chest and two more sets of hands locked around my thighs, holding me spread wide and open for fucking. I felt a cock nudge at my entrance, the metal ring slide over my sensitive flesh as I was stretched open and slowly filled. The curve of the ring brushed over the sensitive spot inside me that had been awakened by my mate's fingers. My pussy was so swollen and tight, so sensitive that I couldn't help the groan that escaped.

"So full," I whispered, my mouth dry from crying out my earlier pleasure.

I had no idea which man was fucking me, and for some reason that made me hotter than I'd ever been in my life. A mouth claimed mine in a searing kiss. It wasn't gentle, it wasn't tame. I turned my head to the side to meet his mouth better and his tongue slipped inside. I tasted him. He was sweet and musky and delicious. I tried to lift my hands and curl them into his hair, to discover who fucked me, who kissed me, who suckled my breasts.

I was denied. Strong hands grabbed my wrists and held them above my head on the bed as his brother pounded into my pussy with his huge cock, fucking me until my head thrashed from side to side and I begged them to stroke my clit, to make me come again, to give me some relief.

The man fucking me moved his hands to the backs of my thighs, taking over the job of holding me spread wide and open so the others could cup my breasts, pull and tug at my nipples. Hands gripped my ass, widening me for his brother's fucking, hard fingers digging into my flesh and holding me exactly where they wanted me. I didn't know who was fucking me and they'd been right; not knowing made this easier.

The sounds of fucking filled the humid air, the wet slippery sound of a cock sliding in and out of my pussy. Their heavy breathing mixed with my sighs and cries of pleasure.

"She's so tight." Those words had me clenching down on the cock deep inside me. The metal ring stroked over me, my own clit ring being nudged each time I was filled. I was going to come again. It felt different this time. More. I wasn't even touching myself, which was remarkable. I'd come twice against my mate's mouth and I would again… very soon, from being fucked.

"It's… oh, God, it's so good," I breathed into the hot mouth kissing me.

"Come, Leah. I want to feel you come all over my cock." The loud demand reached me from the man fucking me, his command harsh and insistent.

It didn't take more than that. The words set me off and I arched my back as I came again, my other mate's mouth swallowing my cries of pleasure. The cock filling me didn't relent, only moved faster but in a wilder rhythm. He pumped one last time, held himself deep inside as I caught my breath. When I felt his cum coating the walls of my pussy, filling me with one hot, long gush, I came again. I could feel his seed, hot and spurting deep inside, and the sensation of being bathed was too intense.

Seconds later the hands holding my thighs up and back relaxed, the cock inside me slowly pulled out as my other mate's attention shifted to my neglected nipple, tugging and sucking as I moaned, shocked as the need built inside me again, even faster this time. A gush of seed followed my mate's cock, escaping my pussy to drip down over my ass.

I panted and tried to lower my legs to the bed. I didn't have a chance.

"We're not done, Leah." The mate kissing me switched positions with his brother to take his place between my thighs. As his thick cock filled me anew, I squirmed, desperate to escape the sensations overwhelming my body. I hadn't had a lover in quite some time and these men's cocks were huge. I was unused to such eager and thorough attentions.

"Stop moving." My mate took his place at my side, his hand sliding to my throat in a move that made me shudder in surrender. His brother bit my nipple, his hand holding my wrists above my head as a huge cock bottomed out inside me, pressing against the entrance to my womb with an edge of pain.

He pulled out and slammed deep, his balls striking my ass and the top of his cock hitting my womb like an explosion inside me. My pussy was on fire from the first mate's seed, the chemicals they'd talked about rushing through my system like a lightning bolt. I should have thought that very notion absurd, but I couldn't deny it. I couldn't move. I couldn't think.

He fucked me hard and fast, no finesse, just raw animal power that pushed me over the edge in a rush that left me screaming. Then he, too, pulsed inside me, his huge cock filling me with more seed, more pleasure.

Oh, my God, I was going to die from orgasms.

He left me then, and I knew I wasn't done. The hold on my hands released and I bit my lip, waiting for the third cock to fill me. Instead, I gasped as I was flipped easily onto my stomach, a pillow shoved beneath my hips so that my ass was up in the air.

"I don't think I can take anymore," I murmured, the coolness of the blanket refreshing on my cheek and sensitive nipples.

A sharp crack filled the air before I felt the sting on my ass. I jolted in surprise, but a cock slipped between my dripping folds and slid deep inside, pinning me in place.

"You spanked me!" I didn't know which brother I was yelling at.

"You'll take everything we give you."

Flipped the other way, the ring in his cock stroked over a different part of my pussy and elicited new sensations. This brother wasn't gentle, but I was so slick with seed and my own arousal that he didn't need to be. He fucked me hard, his hips slapping against my ass. A hand stroked over my hair, another down the long line of my back. Fingers once again gripped my ass, kneading the soft flesh and pulling my core open wide for his use and pleasure.

I was on the verge of coming again, lost as I was to everything but the hands that touched me, the cock that filled me, the arousing words they murmured. It was the finger that brushed over my back entrance, at first gossamer soft, then pressing harder, that pushed me over the edge. Slick from the seed that coated me, it slipped right inside me as my whole body at first tensed, then relaxed into the pleasure that consumed me. A scream lodged in my throat, the sound trapped with the breath in my lungs. My fingers gripped the bedding, that and the hands that held my ass the only thing that kept me grounded. I was lost, flying away.

I'd never had anything in my ass before. But less than an hour on Viken and I had a cock in my pussy with a finger sliding in and out of my ass. I clenched down on both, trying to hold them inside, perhaps even pull them deeper. I felt the cock in me thicken just before I felt another burst of seed fill me. He groaned—I didn't know who it was—and surely there would be bruises on my bottom from his hold.

A hand once again tangled in my hair, pulling my head from the bed and forcing me toward his brother, who stole my air with his kiss and shoved his tongue into my mouth just as the cock in my pussy shoved in and out of me, leaving nothing untouched. Nothing sacred. Nothing mine. This body was not mine. It belonged to them, to my mates.

My body was sated, beyond replete, but somehow they

forced me to come again, a soft rolling orgasm that surprised me. I moaned at the never-ending waves of pleasure that flowed through me.

Slowly, the cock that filled me pulled out, the ring sliding once again over sensitive tissues. The finger pulled from my ass. I was left blindfolded as two large hands held me in place, softly petting my back. I was content not to move, feeling well used, yet their continued attentions comforted me.

"Good, the seed is staying in."

I was too exhausted to even think about what they were saying. My eyes slipped shut as their hands caressed my skin, as if they couldn't stop touching me.

"Do you think this seed will take root?"

"It can't be that easy, can it?"

"The seed power is already working. She came when we did. Every time. The connection is strong."

"It is her body pulling the seed into her womb."

"Let's keep her hips elevated for a while."

"We do not want her to lose a drop."

I couldn't tell who spoke, nor did I care. I fell asleep without a concern. I had three men who wanted me, who liked me and were eager to fuck me. Perhaps being on Viken wouldn't be so bad.

CHAPTER FIVE

Lev

While we didn't sleep as she did, we continued to sit on the bed and touch her. Each of us dressed in turn while the other two remained with her. By tacit agreement, we didn't want to leave her alone, untouched, even for a minute. I could feel the connection we now shared keenly. It was as if a part of me, which I hadn't even known was lost, had been found. The idea of her being separated from me was too appalling to consider. While the seed power had evolved in our race to bind a female to us, the strength of its effect on me was enough to make both my chest and my cock ache. My cock throbbed, ready to take her again.

But that would have to wait. Whether it was the transport from Earth or the fucking, she was exhausted. Her red lashes fanned pale cheeks as she lay on her stomach, ass raised in the air. Red handprints marked her pale skin, a temporary sign of our dominance.

It was difficult not to take her again, for her lush ass and very pink, very swollen pussy were on perfect display. Only a little bit of seed clung to her folds. Keeping her hips elevated had certainly worked in keeping our mixed seed deep inside her womb to ensure not only that she would be bred quickly, but that the seed power would overtake her. I wanted to stroke my cock again, to take it in hand and release my seed onto her pale skin, to spread my essence and my scent over every inch of her body, to make her mine and mine alone.

But that would not make her happy; she needed all three of us to fuck her, to mark her with our seed. She liked being taken gently. She liked having her pussy eaten. She liked a hard fuck. She was indeed matched to all three of us. I could see the same raging desire, the same protective urges in my brothers that I now felt for this woman. She had reacted to each of us in turn, a wild and wanton lover, eager for all three of our cocks. We would each die to protect her, and that was not a vow a warrior took lightly.

Shouting from outside the building was the first indicator that something was not right. We tensed, our postures ready, our minds shifting focus to possible danger. Drogan went to the window and looked out. "Arrows. They are firing arrows." The first explosion woke our mate and she shifted on the bed. Drogan spun on his heel and stared at me, his eyes narrow, his jaw clenched. "Why the fuck is Sector Two attacking Viking United?"

He strode from the window to stand before me, his jaw clenched as tight as his fists.

"We aren't. We wouldn't." I took a step closer to Drogan. I wouldn't be intimidated.

"Then why are there hundreds of stealth arrows in the air, seeking human targets? Why are your explosive teams firing on the buildings here?"

I went to the window to confirm his words. Sure enough, those were stealth arrows used specifically by my sector.

"Sector Two is the only sector that uses programmable stealth arrows," Tor growled. "What are you trying to do? Get out of the mating? Kill one of us? Or keep Leah—" he jerked his chin toward our mate, "—all to yourself?"

Leah stirred again, but didn't fully wake. It showed just how hard we'd used her. Even being gentle, taking on three men was exhausting. Now, with a threat upon us, she looked entirely too soft, too vulnerable.

"If you didn't want to do this, you should have said so before we fucked her," Drogan added.

I stormed back to the window with Tor following. A swarm of black arrows hovered in the air, waiting to strike at any movement on the ground. Several of them were black with red tips, and would explode on impact. But they were not my arrows, not my men firing them. "Why would I do this? If I had wanted a mate, I would have said so. Neither of you would have protested in the beginning."

"Yes, but that was before we saw her, before I fucked her," Tor commented, glancing over his shoulder as Leah stirred. "My seed's inside her now, just as yours is. She is mine, and I will not give her up."

She woke with a small yawn and rubbed her face, then realized how exposed she was. With fumbling hands, she shifted up onto her hands and knees, tugging the blanket up around her body. Frustrated with the pillow she'd been resting upon, she tossed it out of the way.

With her body mostly covered, her hair tousled, and her pale flesh still pink from our attention, she looked more decadent and desirable than ever. The white sheet only emphasized the pale glow of her soft skin and the dark silken blood-red color of her hair. She looked around the room, holding the blanket to cover her breasts. "What's going on?"

"Sector Two is attacking Viken United."

Her eyes widened as she slid off the bed and walked over to us. "What's Sector Two?"

She was covered from her chest down, only her slim leg peeked out as she walked. Her shoulders were bare, and I longed to kiss her there. Drogan grabbed her and pushed her behind him. "Stay away from the window."

"It's not fucking Sector Two," I repeated. I ran a hand

through my hair. "Think, brothers. We didn't know the reason for the regent's request until we got here. He told all of us together just before her transport."

"What's Sector Two?" Leah repeated.

"It's where I'm from."

Tor and Drogan paused and I pushed my advantage. At least they were listening. It's more than would have happened before we'd shared a mate.

"Why would I plan something like this? Think strategically. Arrows are obviously Sector Two. If this were my attack, I'd be sure to use something else to deflect blame. Perhaps one of you has planned this and intends to implicate me."

They glanced at each other.

"Someone is pretending to be from Sector Two to keep us at each other's throats," Drogan said.

That's what I assumed. "If we are fighting each other, then Leah can't be bred. The alliance of our three sectors would fail."

We all glanced at our mate, tousled and well fucked where she peeked out from behind Drogan's broad back.

"She could be with child now," Tor commented. "We put enough seed in her."

"Bred?" She stepped out from behind Drogan. "What do you mean by bred?"

Clearly women on Earth were not bred like on Viken.

"You are to deliver the one true leader of Viken," Tor told her.

She came out from behind Drogan all the way. "So you fucked me because I'm a brood mare, because you want a child for some stupid alliance, and not because you wanted me?"

Hurt mixed with anger tinged her words. I saw the crushing defeat in her eyes and in the way she slumped her shoulders.

"I do not know what a brood mare is, but it does not sound good. We wanted you, Leah," I said, taking a step closer. She retreated, looking away.

"God, men are the same wherever they are," she grumbled. "I left Earth to get away from an asshole who wanted me as a possession and now I've got three of them."

"We do not have time at the present to explain ourselves," Drogan told her. "This is bigger than the regent's plan, unless he knew of a deceit by the rebel factions or some new enemy."

"An enemy who is pretending to be from Sector Two," I said.

"Then we agree to work together?" Tor looked between us and we gave each other identical looks. Frustration, anger, protection.

Protection. That was it. "They want Leah."

Tor and Drogan paused. "That would be an excellent reason to want us at each other's throats," Tor added.

"Who?" she asked. "Who wants me?"

Besides the three men matched to her? Besides the three men who'd fucked her and given her their seed? Besides the men whose seed power she would soon crave?

"We don't know, but it is our duty, our privilege, to keep you safe," Tor told her.

"Yes," Drogan agreed.

"We fear you might be the target of a faction of rebels who wish to keep the planet divided, who does not wish for you to carry the one true heir," I said.

Tor went to the window, then lowered the blind. "We must separate and leave Viken United."

Viken United was neutral territory. A small town located on an island, it allowed for all sectors to attend peaceful meetings. It was rare that representatives from the sectors met; I'd never met my brothers before today. Perhaps it was because we were identical or because we now had a common goal, especially with the seed power upon us, that I felt our differences slip away. Our focus before now had been to be good and responsible leaders in our sectors. But now? Now we stood together for Leah.

"Yes, we can meet again, someplace neutral, someplace no one will recognize one of the three sector leaders or their mate." I paced as I spoke, Leah watching us with wary and hurt eyes.

"A Viken bride training center?" Tor made the suggestion, and the more I thought about it, the better the idea sounded.

"A fuck hut?" The nickname stuck as every male on the planet knew exactly what happened in the isolated huts built on the grounds of the training center. Women were trained, spanked, and fucked into submission. The idea of taking Leah there, of having her tied, her ass in the air for my hard spanking, her legs spread wide for my cock... I had to shift my cock in my pants at the thought. In Sector Two, we dominated our women, saw to their every need and darkest desire. We made sure they never looked to another, never needed another, never had a secret fantasy that went unfulfilled. I couldn't wait to discover the dark fantasies lurking behind Leah's innocent eyes.

The Vikens built mate training centers that were often used by warriors upon their return from the front lines of the war with the Hive in deep space. Viken warriors served on the interstellar battleships, fighting the Hive, as warriors from all member planets did. While they had been sending less than in the past, agile and skilled men were still on the front lines. Warriors lucky enough to earn commendation and the rank of an officer were granted brides by the coalition program before they returned home. The mating centers provided much needed privacy, security, and the equipment necessary to train a new bride.

"They will be looking for the three of us with Leah," Drogan said. "So we will give them just one man and one mate."

Tor understood right away. "Being identical is certainly useful."

Leah looked confused, but remained silent.

Drogan went to the bathing room and returned with

scissors. "Lev, it is your sector that is being impersonated, which means you should take Leah. It will appear as if we believe they are Sector Two arrows and you are taking her home."

"Yes, a good point," I agreed.

"No," Leah said, looking at the floor, then glancing between us. She didn't look confused any longer, but clear and focused. "I don't know what's going on, but if I'm going to get answers from the three of you about this whole breeding thing, we have to get somewhere safe first, right?"

We nodded.

"Then I have an idea," she continued.

"We are eager to hear this," Drogan said, crossing his arms over his chest.

Leah smiled. "A shell game."

I didn't know what the hell a shell game was, but I knew when she explained that our mate wasn't only beautiful, she was also smart and cunning. A ruthless combination that matched the three of us perfectly.

• • • • • • •

Leah

I had no idea what was going on. None at all. The men mentioned arrows being shot and I was confused. Arrows! Between the long dress and the outdated weaponry, I thought I'd landed in Sherwood Forest and not on Viken. Curiosity got the better of me and I wanted to see these arrows, but Drogan would have no part of that. He'd pushed me behind him, blocking me from the window. At first I was bothered by his caveman ways, but I realized it was because he was protecting me, shielding me from harm with his body.

I didn't understand their talk about sectors, but I did understand politics. My father had been a high-ranking city councilman before he died and I'd listened to many dinner conversations where deals were made and contracts signed with handshakes. I'd followed in his footsteps for a time, serving as a low-level city clerk, eager to work my way up the ranks and eventually run for office. But that had been before meeting my fiancé. He'd convinced me to quit my job, to become more dependent on him. That should have been my first clue that something was wrong.

Here and now, on this alien world, someone was trying to get to me through the three men, dividing them, not geographically, but by rousing suspicion and playing on old distrust. It seemed to me that their bond as brothers was stronger than that of whatever sector they came from. Perhaps it was the unbelievably strong feelings I had for them. I'd known immediately when I stood before Drogan in that line of men that he was my match. But now, the feeling was even stronger.

The pull I felt to these three men was intense. I needed them, I needed their touch and their seed, which was absolutely insane. Their seed! I felt like I was craving a drug. They'd mentioned seed power and I had no idea what that was either. I had so many questions, but it wasn't the right time. We needed to get away from those with the arrows and I had an idea. Fortunately, they weren't too Old World to listen. After I told them, they smiled, satisfied with the plan.

Drogan handed the scissors to me and knelt on the floor at my feet. "Cut it to match Lev's," he said.

On his knees, he was at the height where I could easily trim his long hair. I cut it, then Tor's slightly longer locks to match Lev's. It didn't take long and soon enough the three looked the same, except for the scar in Lev's eyebrow. But that difference was indeed small. From a distance, it would not be evident at all. They changed clothing, Drogan leaving for a moment to return with black attire identical to Lev's. Tor and Drogan changed into the new clothing and when the three stood before me my jaw dropped in shock. They were, indeed, identical. But I could tell them apart now. I sensed them: Lev's darkness, Tor's anger, Drogan's pride. They each pulled me, their seed power a unique taste on my senses, but each one I craved.

I'd known them for less than two, maybe three hours and I knew all of this. It was crazy. Everything was crazy since I arrived. But the slick feel of their seed sliding down my thighs was like a drug and it seemed I liked crazy very much.

When Lev held up my dress for me, I realized I'd done all the hair trimming in just a sheet. It wasn't until then that I took note of my body. I wasn't sore, really, but I felt very well used. My pussy ached and I noticed my clit again, the ring through the hood a constant tease. It was true, it made me eager for more. Being fucked by three men, one after the other, wasn't enough. I wanted more. Again and again.

"Ready?" Tor asked.

I nodded as the other men stripped the bed and put together the decoys.

"We will take to the water and meet this evening," Lev said.

Drogan nodded. "Take her, Lev. Remain in the fuck hut until we reunite and have time to consider our next steps. But do not fuck her, brother. Until she is bred, we must share her each time."

Lev wrapped the sheet about me and lifted me into his arms, not giving me the time to think about the idea of being bred. It felt good to be held by him, as if I were coming home. Drogan leaned in and kissed me swiftly before tucking the sheet over me completely.

"Wait," Tor said. He lowered the sheet, kissed me as well, and covered my face again.

I couldn't see what happened next, but was reassured in Lev's arms. The sound of voices carried once we were outside and there was shouting, then Lev ran. I was laid down onto something hard, but the ground swayed. All at once I was moving, gliding. I couldn't make sense of it, until I heard the sound of water lapping. A boat. I remained quiet and still until Lev murmured. "You may remove the sheet from your head, but don't rise until I know we are away safely."

While I couldn't say that the plan had worked—Drogan and Tor each carrying bundles of pillows wrapped in sheets as decoys—we were away from danger. If the group wielding arrows had an allegiance to a specific brother, they would be afraid to kill him. How the other brothers had escaped, I didn't know. I just knew that we would be together again soon. My body ached, craving all three of my men, and I felt as if I had to have them with me again or I'd die.

Pushing the material out of my face, I breathed deeply of the moist air. The sky was blue and dotted with clouds. If I didn't know any better, I would have thought I was still on Earth. It was the two moons in the sky that reminded me that this was a new home, a new life. I looked down my body and saw Lev with an oar. Every time he lifted it, water dripped from the wooden blade. We seemed to be in a wooden canoe, for it explained the gliding feeling and its long narrow shape. I could smell the water, the salty tang that filled the air. I spent long minutes quietly watching the man who had just fucked me. My pussy ached from their virile attentions. Had he fucked me first? Had he pounded into me holding my thighs wide, or had he flipped me over and taken me from behind?

I had been blindfolded and had no idea who had done what to me. It was the three of them, together, who had taken me. It didn't matter whose cock filled me, they'd all fucked me. But for some reason, I wanted to know which touch belonged to him, which hard cock had been his.

I studied him. The resemblance between the three of them was remarkable. The strong jaw, the shadow of whiskers that covered it. They hadn't given me the chance to touch them, but I wondered if they would be soft or scratchy beneath my palm. His eyes were dark, much darker than his hair. Tanned skin indicated that he spent a lot of time outdoors. The scar that bisected his brow was evidence that he had seen danger. The way the three of them did not panic when the attack came added proof. These men were warriors.

"You all fucked me out of duty alone," I said, my voice quiet. "None of you wanted a mate." I was quickly turning into a hot mess. My emotions were shifting so quickly that I was roiling inside. Confused, hurt, needy all at once. So much had happened to me in only a few hours—and I didn't mean just being fucked by three strangers—that I was overwhelmed. If I were on Earth, I'd say I was hormonal. Here, perhaps it was that odd seed power. Either way, some enemy I didn't even know was trying to take me, for a dark purpose I could only imagine. For my mates, I was just a baby machine, and that was all.

Lev's gaze shifted in all directions, probably watching for any possible danger. He didn't look at me as he answered. "Viken is a complicated place, Leah. There have been decades of war and a very tenuous peace. My brothers and I, we are the true leaders of Viken. Separated as infants, we were used to maintain this peace, but at the cost of a divided planet. It is you, and our child, who will bring all Vikens together once more."

I was lying in a wooden canoe—a simple canoe—and I held that much power in my womb? Right. How could I, simple Leah from Earth, hold such power? And I noticed that he hadn't answered my question.

"You did not want me, Lev. Not one of you wanted me. You simply wish to save your world by breeding me." Surely he could hear the disdain in my voice at that word.

I'd wanted children, someday, but not because a child was needed for planetary harmony. I wanted to have a child with a man—not three—who longed for the sleepless nights, the first steps, the milestones of watching a person grow from a helpless infant into a full grown adult, as much as I did. I wanted my child to be a creation of love, not political gain.

His gaze met and held mine. "No, I did not want a mate." While he didn't deny it, it didn't lessen the sharp pain of his words. "All three of us were summoned to Viken United today under false pretenses. You were dangled in front of us like a special sweet. The last time my brothers and I were in the same room together was when we were four months old."

"And you were separated, sent to grow up in the various sectors?" I asked, remembering bits and pieces of their words from earlier.

I couldn't imagine that, being separated from siblings like that, and for political reasons. I'd heard of identical twins being able to read each other's thoughts. I'd heard they couldn't be apart, that it hurt them somehow. I'd even heard they knew the moment their twin died. But triplets separated so young? I ached for them. Perhaps I wasn't the only one sacrificing.

Lev nodded. "When our parents were murdered." He switched the oar to the other side and the boat turned slightly. "Our separation has kept the peace, saved many lives. But not enough. It is not enough. Now we focus on killing each other instead of protecting the planet. Our warriors have grown complacent and forgotten the true danger to our people. You will remind them. Our child will unite them."

"How can you believe that? You three came together for me just a few hours ago and already the fighting has started."

He tilted his head and looked at me. "There was always strife, but the power you will hold is enormous. And there are those among us who do not wish for peace."

"How am I powerful?" I asked, asking what I'd previously thought. "I'm just a woman from Earth who left because—" I bit my lip, not wanting to share with him how weak I really was. If I was the woman, the link that joined these men together to make a baby, the mother of a new life destined to be the leader of an entire planet, he didn't need to know I was such a loser for being engaged to such a dangerous and evil man, for believing his lies.

"You hold great power because we chose to give it to you," he replied.

I frowned. "I… I don't understand."

"I'm coming to see now that our mating was never truly a choice. The connection between mates is too strong. You felt it when you came upon Drogan in the line of men."

I couldn't deny that.

"But it is the seed power now connecting us that makes the four of us dangerous to those with less than scrupulous plans."

"I heard you saying that before. Seed power?"

"The seed from a Viken's cock, when it touches his mate, when it fills her pussy, it unites him with his mate in elemental ways. It changes our bodies on a cellular level, as it will change yours. I know you feel the pull between us, the aching need, the addictive force."

I shook my head, refusing the truth. Changed me on a cellular level?

"How *do* you feel?" His gaze raked over me and I flushed, glad he could not see my nipples hardening, my pussy clenching. When I remained silent, he stared at me, his eyes dark but tranquil pools of authority. I could drown in his eyes, forget myself and get lost there.

"Leah, I am the brother who will tie you up and take what I want from you. I will be the one to toss you over my knee and spank your ass for being naughty."

My mouth fell open and I felt fear roar to life. So, I'd done it again? Trusted an asshole who would hit me, who would—I couldn't even think about it. "You… you will beat me?"

"Beat you? Never." He shook his head slowly. "I will demand obedience. I will also give you pleasure. Exquisite pleasure. I will watch your pulse and your breath. I will know when you lie, when you try to hide, when you truly need to come and when you would simply let your body rule you."

It was my turn to shake my head. "No."

"You wouldn't be matched to me if you didn't want me to own you, Leah. Imagine me tying your wrists to the headboard so I can have my way with you. Imagine me sliding my cock into your ass instead of my finger. Imagine me withholding your release until you scream, until you lose control. Until I command you to come all over my cock or my tongue."

So Lev had been the one to take me from behind, to twist his finger in my virgin bottom hole, to fuck me hard, to the brink of pain before making me explode? Oh, God, I was equally mortified and aroused.

"The seed power doesn't just affect you. It affects me as well. Tor and Drogan, too. They are feeling it more keenly now, surely, for they are not near you. Tell me. How. Do. You. Feel?"

Each word was clipped and intense, the sharp edge of it making me reply without thought.

"I don't know *what* I feel exactly. Longing, need, arousal. Ache."

"An ache for our cocks?"

"Yes, but an ache because… because they are not here."

"Tor and Drogan?"

I licked my lips, worried he'd think I wanted the others instead of him. "Yes. I… I miss them."

"Good girl."

"You won't spank me or tie me up?"

His eyes narrowed. "I'll do both and you're going to love it."

I didn't know what else to say, nor did I want to continue to wonder why I was so fascinated, so aroused by his very dirty plans even after all that had happened to me on Earth, so I switched topics.

"Where are we going?"

"To a remote center used to train new mates. Most mates aren't matched as we were, but many warriors return from the fighting and they are unfamiliar to each other. For some mating to succeed, a retreat to a center can help. This specific center is the most remote, most isolated one. It is for the most recalcitrant of Viken females."

"You think I'm recalcitrant? Seriously? I'm from Earth, not recalcitrant," I muttered. He was not very skilled at wooing. Not much of what he said—my mood, his interest in tying me up—endeared me to him. Even so, I wanted him with a ruthless need that I could not deny.

"You were quite accepting when we fucked you earlier, but you have more to adjust to than the average Viken female with a new mate."

"Oh? Like what?"

"To begin with, you were not a virgin, therefore we must break you of any past connection."

"I assure you," I grumbled, thinking about my Earth lovers, who, after the bout of fucking I just had, I could now say were most definitely duds. "There are no past connections. Do you think I'd be here on another planet if there were?"

"We do not know of this, just as you do not know us. Even with the seed power, you will be obliged to meet all three of our sexual needs, needs you've been matched to, but as you've just so proven, will most likely deny."

"I haven't denied you anything," I countered. "I fucked three strangers within minutes of my transport." As mortified as my mother would have been with me—she'd have rolled over in her grave if she knew—I'd loved every minute of it. I stared out over the horizon to my right, watched the two large moons begin to rise like silent, golden discs in the darkening sky. A handful of stars appeared among the clouds, but I did not recognize any of them. The heavy weight of water in the air grew colder as their large orange sun set to my left, the chill seeping through the blanket to give me goosebumps. I felt my nipples pebble, but ignored them. I did not need that kind of distraction right now, not with Lev staring at me like he wanted to pounce on me and fuck me senseless.

He angled his chin in my direction. "Remove the sheet and lift your dress. I want to see your pussy."

Staring at him wide-eyed, I screeched, "What? But it's cold."

"I thought you would not deny me. If you do not wish to be punished, obey me now. Show me your pussy."

While I liked that he was eager for my body, I wasn't ready to go there, so I asked instead, "Aren't people going to wonder about identical triplets wandering around this so-called recalcitrant mate center?"

Lev raised his eyebrow, sighed, but answered my question. "They won't see three men; they'll only see one. No one there knows who we are, no one knows that we are triplets. I assure you, everyone at the center will be… preoccupied with their own interests."

I could only imagine what they would be preoccupied doing. Fucking. Tying women down and making them scream with pleasure. Making them beg. My clit pulsed around that tiny ring at the idea.

"We won't go out in public together as a group," he continued. "You will be with one of us at all times, but the four of us will only be together in the confines of our fuck hut."

"Fuck hut? *Seriously?* Is this world so primitive?" I felt like I'd gone back in time. "I'd always assumed Earth was the least advanced planet, with the most primitive men."

"We are much more advanced than Earth, I assure you. We just choose a simpler way of life."

"Like the canoe."

"Like the canoe," he repeated. "Now show me your pussy."

He was a very focused man.

"What if I don't want to?"

"Your disobedience has already earned you a spanking, so if you refuse further, it will only make the punishment longer."

"You're making me expose myself to you!"

He grinned. "I am. But you are going to like it. I promise."

"You will spank me if I don't do as you say?"

He laughed then, tilting his head up toward the sky exposing his neck, his Adam's apple bobbing. "I'm going to spank you either way, mate." His grin was wicked when he looked at me. It was as if he couldn't wait to do so. I glanced down at his lap. Based on the thick bulge pressing against the front of his pants, he was very eager. "The decision is yours as to whether you want to come when I do it."

He seemed to be a patient man, for I took my time considering. I glanced up at the Viken sky, then at him. His watchful gaze returned as he rowed effortlessly, the muscles in his shoulders and arms shifting as he did so. Water trickled off the end of the oar, the wind blew my hair over my forehead. It was so calm. So simple. But was it?

Yes, I'd let three men take me, but this, this seemed different, more intimate somehow. He wanted this—no, demanded it—and I had to decide if I would give in. My mind was telling me no, but my body, God, my body was saying yes. Perhaps he was a mind reader, for he started talking, even though he kept his eyes on the scenery.

"My cock is rock hard. It could be the seed power, but I want you. Drogan got to taste your pussy and my mouth is watering to do so. I wonder if you're as sweet as I imagine. I've heard that when a female first comes in contact with her mate's seed, the need is powerful. It supposedly fades some over time, but that will take years, if not decades."

Decades of feeling like this? I licked my lips at his decadent words. Wouldn't they get tired of me?

"Your nipples must be hard and your clit... your clit must be engorged and very sensitive with the ring there. I bet every time you shift, the ring makes you more desperate to feel my mouth tasting your pussy."

I flung the sheet off me, too warm wrapped in it and my long dress after his dirty words. A smile curved his lips but he didn't comment on my surrender.

"Your own juices and our seed must be coating your thighs now." He turned his head to look at me. Piercing me as if I were struck by one of those arrows. "Show me, Leah."

I focused solely on him, forgetting all the reasons I shouldn't be doing this. I worked the length of my dress up with my fingers, a little at a time.

"Part your legs for me."

I lay facing him, so I spread my legs and lifted my feet onto the bench seat in front of me. As I pressed my knees to the side of the boat to make sure I was spread open and ready for him, the cool air moved over my pussy.

His eyes narrowed, his lids lowering. I saw his jaw clench tight and his cock thickened in his pants.

"If I wasn't rowing, I'd have my face between your legs."

A little moan escaped my lips.

"You will place three fingers deep inside your pussy and hold them there until we arrive. You are not allowed to move them, and you are not allowed to come."

CHAPTER SIX

Drogan

It took only an hour to go from being completely rational to insane. One minute the regent told us about a match he'd made for me—us—and the next minute she'd been transported from Earth. The first time I saw her I felt the connection. When I licked her pussy and tasted her, I knew she was mine. But it was when I came inside her, harder than I ever had in my life, that I was doomed. The fucking seed power might have affected Leah, but it damn well messed with me.

We separated when the stealth arrows rained down, our plan to meet up at the fuck hut. The moment we were separated her effect on me became obvious. Leah had gone with Lev in one direction and I'd gone another. Tor a third. I felt the division from her keenly, as if a limb had been severed. I ached inside—besides my cock being hard, my body hurt for her. I knew that Lev would protect her with his life, but until I was touching her again, I would not be whole.

When I arrived at the Viken bride training center, the heavy cover of darkness had fallen. I snuck inside the hut we had chosen and when I discovered Tor already there, waiting, I knew he was just as affected. While we barely know each other—at all—we could commiserate in how we were reacting to Leah, or the lack of Leah.

"If Lev doesn't get her here soon, I may just crawl out of my skin," he said, his voice laced with frustration and a tinge of anger. Since the huts were spaced well apart and the nature of the place was privacy, I did not worry that someone would knock on the door. One half of the complex was used to train new brides, the other half to process brides being sent off-world, to other warriors, other planets. Either way, privacy was maintained.

No one would disturb us, but Tor lowered the window coverings before we lit the lanterns.

"I know. I need to come, fuck, I ache to do so, but I don't think my hand is going to make a difference."

Tor chuckled. "We've grown up to hate each other and it's taken less than a day for us to come together. Someone is trying to drive us apart. We're brothers, yet strangers, and now we ache for the same woman. Shouldn't we be at each other's throats? I should want to kill you for even thinking about fucking my mate. But she's your mate, too."

"Strangely, I don't feel jealous of you." I eyed the man who looked just like me. "If it were someone else, not you or Lev, but an outsider—"

"He'd be dead."

I would rip him limb from limb. "Agreed."

Glancing around the large room, I skipped the basic requirements—food preparation area, bathing room, table and chairs—and focused on the mating equipment. A bench that was specifically used for fucking, allowing a woman to be positioned with her head lowered so any seed that filled her remained inside to not only assist in it taking root, but to ensure the seed power was achieved. Knowing Lev, it would also prove to be a very effective spanking bench.

"Once she gets here, we will teach her the ways of being a Viken mate. The fucking earlier had just been a preliminary, to get our seed on her, in her, so she was protected from someone else claiming her. Here, it shouldn't be too difficult to train her body to accept three men."

"She took us beautifully earlier. If this is how I feel after one fuck, we don't have to worry about breeding her."

I opened a drawer and found a variety of sexual aids the center offered in all of the fuck huts. Dildos, plugs, rope, small chains, paddles, and more. Anything a man might need for his mate. "If she's not already with child, the effort of it will certainly be pleasurable."

Tor only grunted his reply, then shifted his cock in his pants.

Footfalls across the soft ground broke the stillness of the night. Lev came through the door with Leah in tow. The misery I'd been feeling since we parted was gone, replaced by a sense of euphoria, as if I'd taken a drug enhancement. She was in the same plain dress, her hair a wild tangle now. Her cheeks were flushed and she was breathing as if she'd run here instead of arriving by boat.

Tor and I took a step toward her at the same time and she ran to us, wrapping an arm around each of us. Her fingers dug into my back and she was breathing us in, her face pressed into my chest, then Tor's.

The scent of her was like the most powerful aphrodisiac. I couldn't help the groan that escaped my mouth.

Leah pulled back and looked up at us with wild eyes. "I need you both. God, this is crazy, but I need you to touch me."

She tugged at her dress, but since the buttons ran down the back, she grew frustrated.

Tor grabbed her shoulders and spun her about so her back was to him. Instead of working down the line, he tugged at the two sides and the buttons went flying, bouncing off the wood floor. She wasn't hesitant this time.

Tugging, he worked the dress quickly off her body until she stood naked before us.

"When a female is mated on Earth, do you have a training term?"

She turned around and I looked down at her full, round breasts. The pale pink nipples stood at attention and my mouth watered to taste them. Lower, I could see the ring that dangled over her protruding clit.

"Training term?" She was panting now, her breasts rising and falling as she did so.

We stepped closer.

"On Viken, some men bring their mates to a training center because she needs extra time to learn how to submit properly," I said. "It is, of course, different for each couple, but the outcome is the same."

We put our hands on her, surrounding her on three sides, allowing her no escape. There was no escape from the training center, not that we'd let her out of our sights—a perk of having three strong men to watch over her instead of just one. I doubted once the seed power was upon her that she'd want to go far. Just being separated from Tor and me made her frantic.

"Outcome?"

"We bond with you, form a mating union," Tor said, his knuckles caressing the curve of her right breast. Lev cupped her other breast in his large palm, his thumb brushing over the tip.

"Bond?" Her brow furrowed in confusion, but it slipped away quickly when her arousal was heightened. Her nipples were *very* sensitive, it seemed. "What's the difference between a bond and a mate?"

"You were matched to us by the testing. Yes?"

She could only nod, her lips parted as she tried to catch her breath.

"Because of the match, you are our mate. Usually, it is just one man, so when he fucks his mate for the first time, they are bonded. His seed fills her and a chemical reaction occurs, making the connection permanent."

Her skin was so soft, so smooth, so creamy pale, a

81

striking contrast to her fiery red hair.

While my brothers were definitely making her hot, she was still able to listen to me. "You have three mates, therefore in order for us to create a permanent bond, called a mating union, we have to fuck you together. At the same time."

She tilted her chin up so she could look at me. Her green eyes were blurry and lust-filled. "At the same time?" she whispered. "You mean—"

"I'll take your ass. It is a virgin ass, isn't it, Leah?" Tor asked. Sector Two men were known for their interest in ass fucking and it seemed my brother was no exception.

"I'll fuck your pussy," Lev added.

I put my thumb on her plump lower lip and pressed down, opening her mouth so I could see her straight white teeth. Taking two of my fingers, I slipped them into the dark, wet cavern. Her tongue licked the tips of them, swirling over them, then sucking on them. "And I will fuck your mouth."

Pulling my fingers free, I ran them down the center line of her body and flicked her clit ring, making her gasp.

"Now?" she asked.

Lev shook his head slowly. "Now, I will punish you for disobeying me in the boat."

Tor and I stepped back from Leah, removing our touch. A little sound, perhaps of need, slipped past her parted lips.

Lev took her elbow and led her over to the special bench. "This is used for breeding. A man can take his mate, fuck her from behind, and fill her with his seed. She can rest comfortably as she waits the appropriate time, her lower body elevated, for the seed to settle in her womb. She can also be tied down if she is… resistant."

Leah stared at the unusual shape of it. "That's all I am to you? A breeding machine?"

Lev leaned in and kissed her brow. "The regent requested a match through the bride program. It is his plan to unify the planet with a child from all three of us. A child we will make with you."

"Yes, but it's so clinical."

"We will breed you out of duty, but we will fuck you for pleasure," I told her.

She tilted her chin up so her green eyes were on Lev. "Then why can't you fuck me in a bed like normal people do? Or is this how it's done here?"

Lev lowered his head and kissed her. Tor and I watched as she opened for him and their tongues met. Deep and carnal, the kiss continued until she swayed into Lev, gripping his forearms to steady herself.

"We'll fuck you in bed, Leah. And on the table, and up against the wall, too."

"Outside beneath the stars," I added.

"In the bath," Tor added.

"Everywhere. But this bench," he patted the cushioned knee rest, "is also the perfect spanking bench for when you've misbehaved. Take your punishment like a good girl and we'll give you a reward."

Leah took a step backward. "I don't need to be spanked."

"Did you, or did you not, disobey me in the boat?"

Her mouth fell open. "I thought you were joking."

"We don't joke about obeying us, Leah," I said. "There could be dangers and, in order to protect you, we must trust that you will listen, and do so without question. You know nothing about Viken and we must protect you—and punish you—more strictly than we would if you'd been born here and knew our ways. It would be too dangerous to allow you to make mistakes."

She held up her hands to ward us off, clearly forgetting she was naked. Like we'd try to restrain our desire to touch her. Like she'd be able to resist. "All right. I can see how that would be important, especially since I *am* completely unfamiliar with the planet. I will listen to you."

Lev glanced at me, then back at Leah. "That is good to hear."

I scooped Leah up—with a surprised shriek on her part—and set her carefully on the bench. Her torso settled against the long center piece, cushioned with soft leather like the knee rests, and her breasts hung down beautifully on either side. There were hand holds for her to grip, but as I expected, she sat up. With one hand at the center of her back, I lowered her back down and fastened the leather restraints around her wrists.

"I put my fingers inside of me just as you instructed!"

I paused and glanced at Lev. He shrugged. "I did not touch her, but I enjoyed the view of her fingers sunk deep inside her slick pussy. But you did not obey me right away. That is crucial for survival."

"I don't like spanking! I didn't sign up for this." Leah tossed the words at me in an angry little voice as I tied her down. She even tried to kick out at me when I resumed my place behind her, admiring her ass as I waited for Lev to begin spanking her pretty bare bottom.

"You *do* like it," Tor said, watching.

Leah whipped her head around and stared daggers at my brother. "How the hell do you know that?"

"Your pussy is already getting wet." Tor casually shrugged, then shifted his cock within the confines of his pants. "You were matched to us. While you might *think* you don't like it, perhaps based on Earth custom or even from previous experience, your body knows the truth—and the testing recognized it."

"Have you been spanked before, Leah?" Lev asked.

"No!" she screeched.

Lev gave her a gentle swat to her ass as I strapped in her ankles. She wasn't in a happy mood and I worried she'd kick out and hurt Lev, or even herself.

"Let me up, you overbearing Neanderthals!"

I pressed my lips together to keep from smiling. I barely knew Lev, but I knew he would not let that pass—what the hell was a Neanderthal?—without a nice pink handprint on her lovely ass.

CHAPTER SEVEN

Leah

How dare these men do this to me? I was tied down to a spanking bench—just like in the dream from the processing center! Was this real life? Because it was literally out of this world. I was being dominated and overpowered by alien triplets. One of them was going to spank me and then give me a reward. What kind of reward? Would I get his huge cock deep in my pussy again? Would they blindfold me and take turns? Lev said—

Lev struck my bottom with his hand and a flash of stinging pain raced through my system. I cried out, then lowered my head as heat rushed through me after the sting faded. Heat. Lust. Desire. God, I was so messed up. I wanted him to do it again.

I knew I was wet. I was *always* wet since I'd met my mates. Just the light smack that Lev had given me had made my pussy clench and wetness drip down my thighs. How did I know this for sure? One of the brutes was sliding his fingertips through the slippery wetness right now.

"Your body doesn't lie," Lev said. I heard him lick his fingers, but couldn't turn my head around enough to see it.

In fact, all I could do was look at the plain white wall in front of me. That is until Tor came to stand before me, opened up his pants, and pulled his cock free.

Smack!

Ouch! I stiffened and tried to shift away from the stinging blow Lev rained down on my ass but there was no way I could move. The heat of his last strike sent a lightning bolt of need to my pussy and my body began to tremble.

"That was for not obeying me immediately. We would be done now, but you clearly need more."

Smack!

"That was for your sass."

Smack!

"That was for denying yourself this. You like to be spanked."

"*I* like seeing your pink handprints on her soft skin." Drogan. He was a cocky bastard. "May I interrupt, Lev? Just for a moment?"

Lev agreed and I tensed in anticipation as Drogan knelt between my legs.

Tor, directly in front of me, gripped the base of his cock and began to stroke himself off. I could do nothing but watch as pre-cum seeped from the tip and formed a bead on the metal ring. I licked my lips, eager to taste it. I was ridiculously desperate for his cock, even though some twisted part of me believed I should hate them for this, hate myself for wanting more.

I cried out as Drogan's mouth clamped down on my pussy. He licked and sucked me, stabbing deep with his tongue until I was squirming and thrashing on the table. I opened my mouth to cry out and Tor used that opportunity to slip his cock into my mouth a couple of inches, just enough to tease me with his pre-cum. The chemicals from his seed hit my bloodstream like searing hot lava rolling through my body. With Drogan's mouth sucking hard on my clit, I saw stars. I was on the edge. I needed to come.

In some kind of silent agreement, both men pulled away

from me, leaving me panting. Begging. God, I was pathetic. I felt like a wild animal, completely out of control. I needed them. I wanted them. In my mouth. In my pussy. In my ass. Everywhere. Anywhere. I needed—

Lev's huge hand stroked my ass like he was caressing his favorite pet and I pushed back into him, desperate for contact. "You will count out your punishment from earlier, Leah. Twenty to start. If you're a good girl, I might let you have more."

Lev began to spank me and each time I gasped at the heat of it, the tingling, fiery burn of it. "One. Two," I counted as I kept my eyes on Tor's cock. Each hard strike shifted me forward on the bench so the ring in my clit made contact with the hard surface beneath me. I whimpered with each strike, the hot burn spreading through my system like liquid fire.

When I got to seventeen, something deep inside me broke open, unleashing a storm of emotion I had no hope of controlling as tears raced down my cheeks. Weeks of fear and worry, nerves and anxiety about having my fiancé find me, poured out of me with each painful strike of Lev's hard hand on my ass. He didn't stop at twenty, and I didn't want him to.

Surrounded by these men, my rational mind shut down and the primitive animal inside me took over. It knew I was safe. Totally, completely safe, and my walls fell. My control slipped. I sobbed. I counted. I begged him to spank me harder, to break me wide open and take my pain and fear away. Even though I was lightyears from Earth, I'd brought my emotions from there with me, like unwanted luggage. I whimpered and pleaded with my mates to own me, to fuck me, to keep me forever.

By the time I reached thirty, sweat coated my skin and my ass was pulsing with heat. My nipples tightened to the point of pain and I was desperate to be fucked. Filled.

I needed to come. I needed them to fill me up.

Lev's swats changed to a gentle stroking, the softest

caress, as Tor stepped toward me. "Open up, Leah."

His cock was inches from my mouth and I could do nothing but do as he said. Nor did I want to.

"Good girl. Now stick out your tongue. I'm going to come all over it."

I watched as he continued to stroke himself before he settled the tip of his cock on my tongue, the hard ring pressing down. He groaned as hot seed spurted to coat the inside of my mouth. I could taste him, salty and hot. With a ragged breath, he stepped back, then knelt down before me.

"Swallow."

I did, then licked my lips. Within a matter of seconds, arousal pumped through me with such intensity that I was about to come. I closed my eyes and groaned, gave myself over to the feeling. Was this what shooting heroin was like? Pure bliss?

"Oh, Lev, please."

"Please, what?" he asked from behind me, his voice dark and rough.

"I need you to fuck me."

I fought against my bonds, frantic to get my hands on a cock. "Please. I need it." My eyes flew open and I began to panic. "It's too much. I need it. Give it to me!" I shouted.

What was wrong with me? I was... desperate. It only became that way after I swallowed Tor's seed. God, this fever was caused by the seed power they spoke of. The thought terrified me for a moment, but then I remembered Lev's explanation. This bond had the same effect on the men. They needed me as much as I needed them.

I felt a hand tugging on my stinging ass cheek, pulling my pussy open wide as a cock nudged my entrance and then thrust deep.

I screamed. That was what I needed. Thick, hot cock. Even the scent of it, musky and dark, was appealing.

Lodged deep inside, Lev leaned over me, sank his teeth into the spot where my neck met my shoulder and pulled his cock back, then rammed himself home. The angle I was positioned had my ass high and his cock slid in perfectly, like a sword in a sheath. I couldn't do anything but take his hard thrusts. Now that he was inside me, I calmed and gave myself over to it.

"I've been hard for you ever since you transported. I don't think my cock will ever go down. Fuck, I'm like a randy youth. I'm going to come."

The wet sounds of fucking filled the air. Tor stroked my sweaty hair back from my face and I saw desire there once again.

"You need cock, Leah? You need us to fill you, to put our seed inside you? Don't worry, we'll take care of you." I looked up and saw Drogan stripping off his clothes, his cock springing free, ready for its own turn.

"Come for us, Leah. Come now." It was Lev who pushed me over the edge right into pure bliss with his cock stroking over every perfect place deep inside me and his palm landing hard across my ass, one cheek then the other, as he did so.

When he came deep inside me, his seed coating the walls of my sex, I came again. I moaned when he slipped from me, but they didn't leave me wanting. Drogan took his turn as Tor played with my breasts, tugging on the hard tips, timing his hard pinches to the deep thrusting of Drogan's hard cock. Drogan reached around to my clit and stroked me easily to another orgasm as he, too came quickly and emptied himself into me.

I was wrecked, wrung out, and unable to calm down. My body's aching hunger for these men was still there, still roaring through my system like a wildfire through dry kindling. Tor left me to take his place behind me, to fuck me, and I couldn't stand the waiting, the emptiness of my pussy a sensual torture I could never have imagined just a few days before.

Instead of putting his cock in me right away, Tor took his time in playing with my back entrance, using his fingers to open me up, to stretch me for a plug that he slid deep and settled inside me. I should have been appalled as I'd never taken one before and I barely flinched at its insertion. It should have hurt or at least been uncomfortable. But the warm glide of some kind of scented oil ensured that I only felt pleasure, dark, carnal lust that built at being touched and played with in this new place. Only when I felt the flared base of the plug keeping my cheeks parted, the thick feel of it stretching me open, did Tor fuck me.

His huge cock filled me and the sensation of being too full made me moan. Instead of backing off, Tor grabbed my ass cheeks, still burning from Lev's hard spanking, and squeezed hard enough to make my pussy flood with new moisture. The pain triggered an avalanche of need, lust, and a reminder that I belonged to them. Forever.

Tor pulled on my ass and the sensation of being spread even wider pushed me into a mindless haze. My body trembled, completely out of my control, and I didn't care. I simply needed the hard pounding of his cock, the soft stroking of Drogan's hand on my back and the hard pull of his hand in my hair. I needed Lev's hot tongue teasing my nipple as he shoved two fingers into my mouth so I could lick the taste of my own pussy from his flesh.

They didn't let me up, didn't stop fucking me for God knows how long. I lost track of time. I lost track of everything. All I knew was that the men were as insatiable as I, their cocks never softening. Even with my hips angled up, their seed slipped from me, long rivulets of it dripped down over my clit and down my belly. The last thing I remembered was being carried in strong arms and laid on a soft bed.

· · · · · · ·

I woke up in the middle of the night, my eyes opening to a dark room, disoriented. My bedroom window, usually on my left, was now on my right. There was no street noise, no hum of my air conditioner. Sitting up, I blinked, then the sleep cleared enough for me to remember. Perhaps it was the hand that moved on my thigh that helped nudge my brain into my new reality.

I was on Viken. I was in bed with three men. I should have noticed it first, their scent. It was almost identical for all three of them, but I recognized each had their own variation. Lev, dark and powerful; Tor, open and confident; Drogan, wild and focused. I was quickly learning their subtle differences in personality—even in the way they fucked. I had thought I would like it just one way, but when each of them had their turn, I'd come for them all. God, had I ever.

I liked being brought to orgasm by just Drogan's face between my thighs. I'd liked being spanked and fucked at the same time. I'd liked being tied down. I'd liked having a plug in my ass. God, I was such a slut for these men!

The things they'd done to me before I fell asleep were probably illegal in several states back home. Here, though, it didn't seem to be anything but normal. The Vikens had created special centers for mates to learn about such things. Embarrassment riddled me, for was it normal to be strapped to a spanking bench and punished? Was it normal to actually like the feel of my stinging, hot skin from the hard spanks from Lev's hand? Was it normal to literally crave three men? Was it normal to enjoy having my ass played with?

I'd never come before without playing with my clit and earlier I'd come over and over again without any stimulation there at all. My body, even now, ached for them.

No, it just ached. My breasts were tingling and my nipples were hard. I didn't have to see them in the dark to know that they were pebbled into tight peaks. Lifting my hands to my breasts, I cupped them and a soft moan escaped my lips. Shifting, my pussy slid over the sheets, the clit ring being nudged. I was aroused, so very aroused that heat crept into my veins and spread through my body.

The rustling of the bedding came just before a light was turned on. Just a soft glow, enough to see by, but not enough to hurt the eyes. What I saw was three men, naked and surrounding me. The sheet that covered us had slipped off me. I, too, was naked, but I only had eyes for my mates' hard bodies.

"Leah?" The voice was rough with sleep. I didn't look to see who it was, for I was too needy.

"There's... there's something wrong with me," I whispered.

The other men stirred and Drogan sat up behind me, his hand on my shoulder. I moaned again at the contact. "She's hot to the touch."

At his touch, I groaned. Without thinking, I laid back on the bed and parted my legs. I should have been ashamed of my slutty action, but I was too far gone to care. As the men sat up to look at me, I grabbed the back of my knees and pulled my legs back and open. "Please," I begged. God, I was begging these men to fuck me.

Glancing down my body, I could see my clit was engorged so much that its hood was pulled back, the little ring away from the sensitive tip.

Lev and Tor glanced at each other. "Seed power," they said at the same time.

"I will eat your pussy until you come again," Drogan murmured against my neck. "Your pussy must be too sore for another fucking after the one you had earlier."

I *should* be sore, very sore, from fucking three men—again and again—but I wasn't. Even so, I didn't really care. My body was telling me it needed cock and it needed it now.

"No," I replied. Turning my head, I looked into Drogan's eyes.

"No?" he repeated. "You will go against us? Didn't you learn from your spanking and plugging earlier?"

I shook my head, licked my lips. "I need more. I need your cocks. I *need* you to fuck me. Your mouth on my pussy, it's not enough."

I looked up at my three men who loomed over me with concern—and desire—on their faces.

"You've succumbed to the seed power, Leah," Tor said.

"I had no idea it was so powerful."

"It is from all three of us, not one," Lev added. "It will be very intense for her."

"Please," I begged, my pussy dripping with their earlier seed and my own arousal. I reached down and slipped my fingers over my folds and pushed them inside. If they weren't going to use their cocks, I would use my fingers. Drogan and Lev each took one of my knees and pulled them wide just like I'd held them as Tor moved to kneel between my thighs. His cock was erect and ready, pulsing up toward his navel.

He took my fingers from my pussy and placed my hand in Lev's, who moved it by my side. He didn't release his hold.

Tor began playing with the plug in my ass, tugging on it, then pressing it deep. Again and again. I tried to move my hips, but Lev and Drogan held me down.

Shifting his hips, Tor lined up his cock at my eager entrance and slid inside of me. It was one slow, easy stroke and I groaned, my eyes falling closed.

"Yes," I moaned, loving the stretch, the overwhelming sense of being full. It was so tight with the plug in my ass. "Fuck me. Please! I need it."

I sounded like a wanton slut but I didn't care. I needed cock and I needed it now.

"With pleasure, mate." Tor began to move, fucking me in earnest as his brothers held me open. "With pleasure."

• • • • • • •

Tor

We were at a training center for more difficult brides, yet Leah was the least recalcitrant of mates. In fact, I'd call her eager, or voracious, or greedy. Having the seed power from three men made her insatiable. While we'd only taken her over the bench with a simple spanking and fucking, the power of it woke her from sleep and we'd had to tend to her again in the middle of the night. The term *tend* included a good hard fucking from all three of us. Leah had insisted on cleaning off our cocks with her mouth, then Drogan inserted a larger training plug into her ass. Only then was she sated enough to fall back asleep. Now, with the dawn, she was still sleeping, but for how long, none of us knew. We were not familiar with having a mate, nor with being together for that matter.

Drogan was preparing a simple morning meal in the food preparation area as Lev and I sat at the small table by the window. A few couples were about, the weather enjoyable. Men and their mates were going about their day, perhaps going to a specific training hut. All things were available here, all desires could be met. Learning to properly wield a crop, or tie a bride with ropes without causing harm. There were classes on pleasing a bride with an eager tongue, or learning to read her body during sexual play. As for the brides, a bride could be taught how to suck cock or even how to train her back entrance for a good fucking. Lev seemed to have mastered the art of reading Leah, knowing what she needed, even if she denied it. I was learning this about her, too. How he'd known she needed the release of a hard spanking, I wasn't sure, but she had. She'd broken and screamed, and through her tears and thrashing had begged for more.

What I longed to do was learn more about how to stretch Leah's ass. She'd taken a larger plug in the middle of the night, but was stretching her open enough to get her ready for my large cock? Lev may want to learn new ways to secure Leah in ropes or take her to a deeper level of submission. Drogan? Hell, he was obsessed with oral sex, but seemed to have that down, if Leah's orgasms were any indication. Anything we needed to learn to please our new bride was available to us here. As long as only one of us was with her at a time, no one would be the wiser to our deception. The only outward sign of our differences was

Lev's scar running through his eyebrow, but with Leah with us, no one would be paying any attention to Lev's face.

I knew I couldn't focus on my surroundings when her nipples hardened right before my eyes.

"Regent Bard was killed in yesterday's attack," Drogan told us both as he finished preparing the meal.

Lev paused with his mug of morning caffeine halfway to his lips. "At Viken United?"

I nodded. "I heard the news in the east. Did you see it happen, Drogan?"

"Yes. After we separated, I headed west. Regent Bard was coming from the transport center. He was with Gyndar when they were ambushed." Drogan scooped food into bowls. "I was some distance away, but the regent was on the ground with a black arrow through his right eye. Gyndar knelt over him to assist, but there was nothing to be done."

"An arrow through his eye? That wasn't just a lucky shot," I surmised. We were warriors. We knew what an intentional kill looked like.

"I saw it happen," Drogan said, as he placed bowls in front of each of us, then went to retrieve his own. "The assassin took aim from a nearby balcony. He was waiting, as if he knew precisely where the regent was going to be. The attack was precise and well executed."

I picked up my spoon, stirred the morning protein porridge. "So, someone wanted him dead. Was the attack on Viken United designed to kill the regent then, or to get to us?"

"Or Leah," Lev added.

No one had an answer.

"We should remain here, in hiding, until Leah is carrying our child," I said. "Perhaps by then we will know more."

"I agree with the regent's plan," Lev added. "He wanted a unified planet. Apart, we were just bickering weaklings from the three sectors. Together, we can rule Viken. Teach our child to be a better man, a better leader than all of us."

Drogan looked at our bride, sleeping peacefully on the

bed. "It will not be safe for her until she has officially been claimed."

Lev set down his bowl with a scowl. "We can't bond with her until she is bred. That would give one of us an advantage in fathering the child."

I swallowed a spoonful of the warm porridge. "Agreed. But as soon as she's carrying our child, we will need to bond with her immediately. Which means we should focus more intently on her ass training. She took to the plug we used last night, even the larger one, but in order for us to have the official bonding ceremony, we need to take her at the same time. It is her tight, virgin ass that delays this."

Drogan agreed. "Yes, politically it is the best way to keep the sectors satisfied, this bonding. It will keep her safe, even if we are separated. On a more personal note, it will keep Leah more satisfied, too, if she's legally bonded to all of the men she fucks. Perhaps then the seed power will diminish some for her. She was insatiable, almost delirious with her need."

"Being from Sector Two, Tor, you're the one who most enjoys a good ass fuck," Lev said with a grin.

I couldn't help but laugh. "And you don't?"

• • • • • • •

Leah

"I do not see the need for this," I whispered to Tor.

He cupped my elbow and led me across the lush field between the various buildings. The men called them huts, but it seemed my idea of that term and a Viken's was vastly different. They were not huts as I'd seen on Earth. They were more like cabins in the woods. Rustic and simple looking on the outside, but well-constructed with modern amenities such as kitchens and bathrooms on the inside. So much was different here. This was a race of interstellar travelers, with spaceships and technological advances I couldn't begin to dream of… yet they chose to live like this. To cook their meals on stoves and bathe in real water when a number of races had devices that would clean them without ever touching a hair on their bodies.

We'd ridden in a simple boat from where I'd been transported from Earth to this *place*. A bridal training center! A training center *for fucking*. The men said it was for recalcitrant mates. I *wasn't* recalcitrant. Hesitant, definitely. Headstrong, absolutely. When Lev had spanked me yesterday for not obeying him in the boat, I'd been stunned. Shocked that he'd actually followed through with his *discipline*. It had hurt!

But it had also given me permission to hurt, to stop bottling up my fear and my pain. I was shocked that he'd spanked me, but even more surprised by my reaction. I liked that bite of pain. I liked being forced to let go. I'd debated for the last couple of hours what I might do to earn another *punishment* at Lev's hands in the future. I'd cried and kicked and screamed, and I'd let it all out, all the poison inside me. I felt free and empty now, no longer afraid or tense. I was wrung out and exhausted by the whole experience, but I knew I wanted to feel that sting again. I was counting on it to help me hold myself together. I was counting on them, my mates, to hold me together, to make me stronger and keep me safe. I was falling in love with them, depending on them, trusting them… and there wasn't a damn thing I could do to stop it.

I had a feeling Lev had gone easy on me, and that there was more, if I wanted it. More pain. More leashed darkness inside me. I wasn't ready to face that yet, but there was something about these men that made me think about things I never had before. They also made me ridiculously horny, eager to fuck and accept sexual needs I had never dared to imagine before coming here, before being matched to three such powerful and dominant men. They were addictive, a drug I didn't want to live without.

They called it seed power, the chemicals in their seed that

made me eager for them. It seemed absolutely ludicrous, but the reaction was hard to deny. Even now, I was dripping wet, my pussy swollen and achy for my men's cocks. I'd woken up in the middle of the night and begged to be fucked. God, I blushed just remembering how wantonly I'd behaved. I had even loved having the bigger plug put in my ass.

Yes, I was not the same woman who had left Earth. I was not that conservative city councilman's daughter any more. I was wild and wanton, and I didn't care. Right this moment, I didn't care.

Tor led me through the huts, his large hand completely enveloping my own in his gentle hold. I wore a new gown, similar to the first that my mates had destroyed in their eagerness to take me, but a different color. The last one had been a rich, vibrant green. This one was a dark, earthen brown that reminded me of a bear's fur. Tor had dressed me to match him. And as he'd walked with me along the well-tended garden paths between huts, he'd told me the cost, in Sector One, of growing up without a family. He'd kissed me like a drowning man desperate for air, and had vowed to never leave me, or the child they were trying so hard to plant in my womb. The vehemence in his eyes convinced me he meant every word.

We walked in silence for a short while, but I could tell something worried my mates. Lev would never tell me what was going on. I knew that. He would simply expect me to trust him to take care of it. Drogan? Well, he would tell me, if I asked, but I already knew he would choose his words carefully. He was the diplomat, the one who kept the peace between them, and he never spoke without considering his words. But Tor? Tor would tell me the truth.

"What's going on? Why are we hiding out here instead of going back to your capital?"

Tor squeezed my hand and tugged me into the shadow of a giant tree trunk where no one would be able to see us from the walking paths. He leaned down, pulling me close to whisper in my ear. "The old man you met yesterday, Regent Bard?"

I nodded. The old man seemed genuine, and happy to welcome me to Viken and my mates.

"He was the Viken regent. He was extremely powerful. The current leader of our planetary government."

"I thought you three were the rulers?"

Tor shook his head, his hands running up and down my back in a soft glide that made me want to melt into him. "Yes. We are royal by birth, but we were separated when we were babies. Before you, none of us would agree to return to Viken United and rule. So, he held a lot of power, and worked to keep Viken involved in the Interstellar Coalition. But he was not the true ruler."

"You said *was*."

"He was killed in the ambush yesterday. By an assassin."

I put my hand over my mouth, thinking of the gentle and honest old man. "Oh, my God."

"Someone wasn't happy with the regent's plans."

"But that plan was us, Tor. He wanted you three to reclaim the throne." I cupped his face with my hand, and I knew the protective anger I was feeling was what made my voice shake. "You and your brothers are the true rulers of Viken."

He nodded. "Our parents were killed when we were infants. Lev, Drogan, and I survived and were split among the three sectors to maintain peace. We were raised separately. Regent Bard got his way. The peace held from that day to this, but it has been tenuous for almost thirty years."

I ran my thumb along his cheekbone and looked into his eyes, feeling a soul-deep connection. He'd told me the day before about his parents' murder, but still…

"I don't understand. You mean you barely know each other?" When he nodded again, I felt a pang of sadness for them. "I have no siblings, but I would hate to know I was ripped from the only family I had for political gain."

He leaned down and placed a chaste kiss on my lips, even as the large hands kneading my ass were anything but innocent. "That is why you are invaluable. A woman matched to all three of us. Bred by all three of us. Delivering of a child made by all three of us. The infant will be the next ruler of a united planet."

"But if they killed the regent, won't they try to kill you, too?" I asked, my eyes wide. If whoever it was wanted to take over the planet, I knew three very sexy men who stood in the way of that goal.

He gave a slight shrug. "Perhaps, but we believe the real danger may be to you. *You* are the one who will give birth to the one true heir. We only have to fuck you and fill you with our seed. You will be the ruling mother. Your child will be heir to the throne of all Viken."

I looked around, thinking men with bows and arrows might jump out and attack us. "Are we safe here?"

He placed his big hands on my shoulders, leaning down so I was forced to look into his dark eyes. "We will never let anything happen to you. You must trust your mates in that. Only one of us will be with you while we remain in hiding here, the other two will remain out of sight, so it appears we are just another newly mated Viken couple."

"Won't you be recognized?"

Tor grinned. "No. Our planet does not broadcast images like some. Here, everything is managed by a strict hierarchy, orders and laws being passed down from the highest-ranking members all the way to the common farmer and soldier. I doubt anyone here has ever seen anyone but the local leadership."

I looked down at the vivid green grass. "Okay. But when I woke up, I heard you talking this morning. What does any of this have to do with training my ass?"

He smiled. I saw it out of the corner of my eye. "There is a ceremony that will make our bond permanent and legally binding. Our seed power will still call you, and us, but after we bond, it will no longer rule our bodies with such strength."

"You mean I'll be able to think about something other than fucking?"

"I hope not." His all too sexy grin was unrepentant. "But without the bonding ceremony, you would crave us your entire life. The craving can be quite severe and has been known to drive unmated females mad."

"You mean I will always be this... desperate?" I didn't like that idea very much. I liked to be aroused, but this... this was too much.

"Not if you bond with us. All three of us. After we claim you, you will still feel the seed power, but it will be much more subdued."

I didn't need to be told more. The seed power currently pushed me to the very edge of my control. My body ached to be filled, to be touched. I craved the touch of my men. I needed it. The idea of being able to think again, to walk without the brush of my own clothing on sensitive skin driving me to distraction, was irresistible. "All right. I will bond with you." I felt my cheeks heat and knew a dark pink invaded my face. "All three of you."

"To bond with us, you will have to fuck all three of us at the same time. I will take your ass, Lev your pussy, and Drogan will fuck your mouth. Only then will the bond be recognized by our people."

The idea of servicing all three men at once, being pressed between them, feeling and tasting their cocks at the same time, made me moan. Tor laughed and pulled me back onto the path. "That is why you must be trained. I do not wish to hurt you. I am big and your ass is tight." We stopped in front of a hut.

"I had a plug inside of me all night long," I pointed out.

As Tor opened the door for me, he continued. "Yes, but the plugs you've accepted in that sweet little ass were both smaller than my cock. We will spend the next hour getting that virgin hole all nice and stretched, ready for me. There's one challenge with this, Leah."

I tilted my head. Only one challenge? It seemed that everything related to my arrival on Viken was a challenge.

"This is a center for recalcitrant mates. This means that a little extra discipline, a little extra level of submission, is expected by the trainers here."

"You want me to resist you?" I licked my lips. "That may be an impossibility based on my... ache."

He grinned then and his eyes darkened. "I love that you are voracious for us. How about this? Pretend to resist. Pretend you are a bad girl." He stroked his finger over my cheek, tucking my hair behind my ear. "Can you be naughty for me?"

"Does it mean I'll get spanked again?"

He tsked me. "Naughty girls should not be so eager for a spanking. You will get a spanking and something quite large to plumb that virgin ass." He leaned in and whispered, "Be sure to resist."

I knew what that meant and so did my pussy, for my juices slid down my thighs in anticipation as Tor opened the door. With a hand at my back, he led me inside. Once through the doorway, I paused and blew out a breath. Perhaps resisting wasn't going to be as hard as I imagined. Accepting my need for my mates was not the same as accepting what I saw before me.

The single room hut was solely for ass training. I started to giggle at the insanity of it—I couldn't imagine something like this on earth—but stifled it behind my hand. A woman was lying flat on her back upon a soft mat. Straps, connected by hooks on the wall behind her, were wrapped around each of her knees to pull her legs back and open, her bottom lifted off the floor. Her pussy was on full display to her mate who knelt between her spread thighs. Since this was the ass-training room, he wasn't fucking her. Well, he wasn't fucking her with his cock. He was using a very large dildo, not in her pussy, but in her back entrance. Her eyes were closed and she was panting, her skin coated in a sheen of sweat. Her mate leaned close, pumping two large fingers in and out of her wet pussy as the dildo plumbed her ass. He lowered his mouth to suck her clit, hard enough that I could see her soft, pink flesh as he lifted and pulled away from her body. Her back arched and she whimpered in a sound I knew all too well, for I'd made that sound myself, just last night, as I begged my mates to fuck me. The woman was close, so close to finding her release. I tensed and closed my legs, squeezing against the emptiness I felt watching her shudder, her entire body shook as he pushed her to the very edge of orgasm before withdrawing both his fingers and mouth to continue fucking her with the dildo in her ass.

Her pussy was slick and dripping and I watched as her muscles tightened and released as she was worked. Fucked. Owned.

The woman screamed her release and I bit my lip to keep myself from crying out with her. I didn't realize I held Tor's hand in a death grip until he squeezed my hand and leaned down to whisper in my ear, "You're next, mate."

"Good morning." I spun about at the greeting. The Viken male who spoke to us wore simple clothing, but his shirt had an emblem on the chest that signified he was a center trainer. "That newly mated couple is just finishing their session."

His comment was timely, for the woman's second deep moan of pleasure filled the room. Tor smirked and the trainer was professional enough to maintain a placid expression.

"By the time you have your mate settled on the training bench, the other couple will be gone."

Tor nodded, then looked to me. "Strip, please."

I looked at Tor warily, then at the bench where I knew my ass would be up and exposed for training. It excited me and terrified me at the same time. Having one of the men play with my ass while we were all touching and kissing and fucking in private was arousing. This, I wasn't so sure about.

"Come, love. We've talked about this. My cock is as thick as your wrist, but it *will* go in that virgin ass of yours."

"But…"

"You have a choice."

I brightened at the prospect. "You can go over the bench and I can work a training plug into you and make you scream your release, or you can go over the bench and, once you have a nice, big plug in your ass, you'll get a spanking before I let you come."

"You can't be serious?"

"A spanking it is."

My mouth fell open and Tor arched a brow. "You can go now, with just a spanking on your bare bottom, Leah, or you can argue and I'll strike your thighs, and deny you release."

The trainer nodded in approval at my shocked expression, but I knew Tor meant every word. I shook like a leaf, blushing a bright pink as the trainer watched me with intense interest, inspecting every inch of skin as I loosened the dress and let it slide down over my bare breasts and hips to pool on the floor at my feet. Once naked, I met Tor's gaze with as much courage as I could manage and walked over to the bench.

"Good girl, Leah," Tor murmured, and as much as I wanted to be angry at this entire situation, his praise spread through me, making my heart melt and my pussy wet. I wanted him to be happy. I wanted to please him.

"She will be an excellent submissive with a little training. You're a lucky man." I heard the trainer behind me and I glanced at him from beneath my lashes, knowing he could see everything, that he would watch everything Tor did to me. That did not make me happy. I did not like the way his gaze darkened with interest as he inspected my breasts, or the way his gaze lowered to linger on the wetness between my legs.

He did not matter. He had not earned the right to look at me. I did not care about pleasing him. He was nothing to me.

With my rising ire, my pussy tightened and I felt my

desire fading. I was not this old man's plaything. I did not belong to him.

"Eyes on me, Leah," Tor scolded and I tore my gaze from the elderly trainer to look at my mate. His eyes were dark with lust as he looked at me, not trying to hide the way my body pleased him. "No one else is here. Do you understand? You will listen only to my voice. You will feel nothing but my touch. This will please me. You are beautiful, and I want him to see you ache for me. I want him to watch you come for me and envy me such a beautiful mate." He stepped close and lifted my face with one hand, pulled me to his hard body with his other hand on my ass. "I want him hard for you. I want him desperate, knowing you're mine, knowing he can never touch what's mine. Taunt him with your beauty, Leah."

Oh, yes. I could do this, make my mate a god in the old man's eyes. On one condition. "You won't let him touch me? I don't want anyone else to touch me. Only you." My heart was in my eyes and I knew it, but I didn't care. My mates could hold me, touch me, own me. But no one else. I didn't trust anyone else, didn't want anyone else.

"Trust me. I don't share." Reassured by his words, I gave him a small nod and I allowed him to lead me to the bench, the front of my thighs and lower hips pressed forward. Tor's firm hand on my back pushed me down onto the padded table before me and I went willingly, my pussy already wet as I replayed what I'd just witnessed on the table next to us. The woman's who'd screamed her release was now wrapped up in a soft blanket of some sort and curled up resting and happy against her mate's massive chest as he carried her out of the hut, leaving Tor and me alone with the trainer.

"Will your mate need restraints?" the trainer asked.

I looked at the wall in front of me. It was covered in hooks, from which varying sizes and shapes of plugs hung down. I gulped, wondering which one Tor would pick.

Tor went to the wall and selected a small plug, something similar in size to one of his fingers, then a much larger one.

Wow, that one was *big*, with bumps and some sort of control switch... did it vibrate?

"Leah will be a good girl and take this plug," he showed the small one to the trainer, "without a struggle, or I will restrain her and work this one inside her." He lifted the monster plug.

The warning was real and it was my choice.

"Here is your jar of ointment. You have enough in your hut?"

"Yes, thank you." Tor placed it on a small table where I could see it and I watched as he coated the small plug in the slick substance. After, he dipped two fingers into the jar and moved around behind me.

"Breathe, Leah."

The cold slide of Tor's fingers over my bottom hole had me squeak in surprise, but I didn't move from position.

"You can never use enough ointment," the trainer commented.

My cheeks flushed as the trainer continued his commentary as Tor worked my back entrance, slowly stretching me to allow his finger to slide in. I panted past the burn of it and began to push back against the single digit as the sensation of being filled with the very tip of him made me instantly aroused. Just as I began to truly enjoy the fullness, the slight invasion, he slipped free.

I cried out my disappointment, but it was short-lived. The hard tip of the small plug pressed against me and slid into me without too much effort. I gasped as it was seated within and I wiggled my hips to adjust, but it wasn't painful. Uncomfortable, surely, but nothing worse than what my mates had used the night before.

Tor came around and squatted down before me so his face was in line with mine. Brushing my hair back from my face, he met my eyes. "Good girl." He smiled and I couldn't help but smile back. "That was too easy though. This is training, after all."

I didn't have time to question his words, for he moved

back behind me.

I assumed he was going to slip the plug out of me, but instead, I felt the other one, the much larger plug, pressed at the entrance of my wet pussy. My legs shook and I pressed my forehead down into the table, my grip on the edges desperate as he pumped softly, sliding the large dildo in and out of my wet core slowly, so slowly. In. Out. The extra stretch of the plug behind me made the second one in my pussy feel impossibly huge. I was full. So full.

Tor worked me with it, fucking me until I dripped with sweat, desperate to come.

"She's very wet," the trainer commented. "You should be very pleased. Arousal is hard for some mates during an ass-training session."

Tor took hold of both plugs and began to fuck me with them, alternating when one slid deep inside, the other sliding almost all the way out. I knew he was mimicking what it would be like when I had two of my men's cocks filling me, but the trainer did not know this. The old man's voice sounded wispy, as if he couldn't quite catch his breath.

"You should fuck her pussy with the plug in her ass. This will make her grip on your cock unusually tight. This will be excellent practice for your mate and will be a very pleasurable experience for you as well."

Tor did not respond with words, but he did fuck me faster with the plugs and I groaned at the sensation, ignoring the other man's droning about training techniques. I didn't care about him. I narrowed my focus to the sound of Tor's murmurs of approval as he played my body, to the wet slide of the plugs as he filled me with them.

I bit my lip, shaking and on the edge when he pushed both of them deep… and stopped.

"Time for your spanking, naughty girl."

If I thought it would spare me, I would have begged, but I knew any words would be wasted. Especially since he promised me the spanking in front of the trainer.

His hand landed on my bare bottom and I clenched my

cheeks as the sharp pain startled me, making my pussy and ass both clench down on the plugs.

Oh, God. More. I wanted more.

There was no holding back my cries as he continued to strike my bare bottom over and over, the fire spreading through me with each hot strike, each sweet sting. I counted because I had to, the numbers in my head were the only thing keeping my mind whole as fire and lust overwhelmed my senses.

Tears slid down my cheeks to smear on the table beneath me but I didn't even try to stop them. They were the only release I had right now. "Please!"

"You want to come?"

"Yes. Please. Please!" My request screamed from my throat as he shifted his stance behind me and pulled both plugs almost completely out of my body. He held them there, their tips just barely inside me as he waited for me to break.

"What do you want, Leah?"

I was past the point of speech, simply pushed back against him, trying to take the plugs back inside me. He only gave me one, my cries of frustration very real as he filled my ass but left my pussy empty.

"If you will give us some privacy, I would like to fuck my mate now, just as you suggested."

"Of course," the man murmured. "The way your mate is responding, my help is clearly not necessary."

Tor continued to work my ass until the door closed. At the sound, he stopped and leaned down over me, covering my ass and back with his hard body. I lay pressed to the table, my body on fire as he covered me. "You should have seen him, Leah. You are so beautiful, so hot, your pussy so wet for me." His hand slid over my stinging ass cheek to cup my now empty pussy and I whimpered. "I'm so proud of you. Every man in the universe will want you, Leah, will want this." He slid two fingers deep inside my pussy. "Want you."

The intimate glide of his fingers in my wet core was like an electric shock to my system. My body bucked beneath him, completely out of my control. I could only grip the table's edge and fight for air.

Tor stood and pulled back, leaving my pussy aching and empty once more. I didn't move, simply waited, knowing I wouldn't be allowed to come until he chose to let me. I nearly cried with relief as I heard Tor's pants hit the hard floor. Seconds later the hot tip of his cock nudged at my entrance. "I'm going to fuck you, now. Hard."

"Yes!" He slid in deep and I cried out.

"I think you like having your ass filled." He pumped into me.

"Yes!" I repeated. The feel of both his large cock and the plug inside me was so tight, so snug. *So hard. So big.*

His pre-cum coated my insides with every stroke of his huge cock and I was lost, wild. He could have slipped that super-sized plug in my back entrance and I would have loved it. My mate, this connection, was sizzling my brain.

"I need it, Tor. Please," I begged.

"You want something bigger in your ass while I fuck you?"

"Yes!" I cried.

He pulled out of me and went to the wall, unconcerned that his cock thrust out slick and shiny with my arousal. He found one and held it up. I gulped, then clenched around the small plug. I moaned at the sight of Tor coating its replacement with a generous amount of ointment.

Carefully, he pulled the smaller plug from me and replaced it with the other one, the ridged, bumpy new one. As he pushed it inside me to the first ridge, he slid his cock in as well, but only an inch. When he worked the second ridge into me, he slid in another inch. He filled my ass and pussy, one slow, thick inch at a time. When the plug's base bumped my bottom and the blunt head of his cock nudged my cervix, I shattered.

My body clenched down on both thick rods, pulling

them deeper into me. Surely Lev and Drogan could hear me from across the center.

Tor fucked me then, hard and fast and I came again and again, so aroused, so needy that I couldn't stop. Every orgasm pushed me higher and higher, a spiral of need that made me claw that table and beg for more, my voice going hoarse as I demanded more.

"Yes, mate. You're squeezing me so hard, Leah, I can't hold back. I'm going to come."

He did then, his hot seed spurting from me, coating my insides with his special seed, triggering yet another orgasm. I struggled to catch my breath and I could do nothing but rest, sated and weak. My mind was weary and lethargic as Tor slipped from me; a hot gush of his seed followed him, slipping down to coat the insides of my thighs.

Tor rubbed his hand over my ass and I didn't protest when he slipped the smaller plug deep inside my pussy. I had no fight, no argument. I was his. Completely.

Tor picked up my forgotten dress and helped me up onto wobbly legs, keeping a hand on me to steady me as he helped me slide the fabric over my body once more.

"Aren't you going to take the plugs out?" I asked as he held the door open for me, the bright sunshine hurting my eyes after the cool confines of the hut.

Tor shook his head. "You're in training, Leah. Plus, I think that Drogan and Lev would like to see what you've been up to."

The idea of flipping up my skirts and showing the other men how I was filled made me come. I gasped and my eyes fell closed as the soft wave of pleasure washed over me. Once it was over, I looked up at Tor. He was staring at me, wide-eyed.

"The seed power is truly impressive. We must hurry, I'm hard again and I'm sure the others need you as well."

CHAPTER EIGHT

Drogan

I didn't need the sight of Leah naked and strapped to the breeding bench to want to pump my seed into her. I grew hard at the sight of her walking stiffly back from her session with Tor. I knew she must have a very large plug filling her ass and couldn't resist either the smile that spread across my face or the thickening and lengthening of my cock. Knowing she was so eager, so willing and obedient to accommodate our needs made me hard as a rock and eager to fuck her again.

Hell, knowing she was only a short distance away was all that kept Lev and me from rushing to her to relieve the strong pull of the seed power. But we had to remain hidden, to let anyone who saw us at the fuck huts believe Leah was just another Viken female with her new mate. In our own hut though, with the privacy screens drawn, we could do with her as we chose.

We spent the week fucking her everywhere but the spanking bench. We only used that apparatus to slip a consistently larger plug into her ass or for Lev to spank her… just because. By the end of the week, all three of us were confident we could take her at once without hurting her, even with the extra arousal the seed power provided. It wasn't just about breeding her, although filling her with seed was no hardship.

Every time one of us took her away from our hut, we reminded her of her need to be our naughty girl. She'd reveled in this, forcing Tor to give her a bare-assed spanking out in the main area where anyone walking by could witness. I'd taken Leah to see a mentor on eating her out. I was quite confident—and so was Leah—that she could respond to my mouth on her pussy, but we needed to maintain the facade.

While she had enjoyed my tongue torturing her for the entire hour, she hadn't been pretending when I told her she would be tied down and spread open for me, her every reaction monitored by the mentor. As I tied one knee open, then the other, she'd resisted, requiring me to spank her before we could even begin. The fact that she came from her spanking alone only added to her humiliation. But I rewarded her quite thoroughly with my tongue and fingers, the mentor praising my mate's ability to submit.

The knowledge that she enjoyed our domination had Lev tying her to the bed or over the table on occasion to assuage her needs. Whatever she wanted, whatever her body craved, we gave her. We pushed her sexual boundaries and pleasured her into exhaustion every night.

"It has been a week, Leah, and we have delayed as long as we could."

We stood over the bed where she lay, resplendent with her red hair and nothing else covering her curves. She sat up, no longer shy about her body.

"Oh?"

"You must be seen by the doctor. All new mates are seen on arrival for any signs of physical problems, but we stalled for you."

"Your breasts are different," Tor said.

Leah looked down at herself. I could see the change, too.

"Her nipples are larger," Lev commented.

We moved as one to sit on the bed, surrounding her.

Sure enough, her nipples were a bright pink and the usually small circles were larger. They didn't tighten into tight little gems as was normal, but remained puffy and full.

"Everything is larger." Lev cupped a breast in his palm and looked to me. I cupped the other and sure enough, it was heavier. Fuller.

Leah's eyes slipped closed as we played.

"We now have reason to see the doctor."

Her eyes opened. "I do not need to see a doctor because my breasts are larger. It's just PMS."

"Larger… and more sensitive," Lev commented, brushing his thumb over the nipple, ignoring me entirely.

We each added the changes we saw—and felt.

"Our seed has taken root," I assumed.

Pride and very heady arousal coursed through my veins. We'd certainly fucked her enough. I felt virile and powerful at the early signs of her being bred.

She shook her head. "It is too soon. As I said, I'm sure it's just PMS."

"I do not know what this PMS is. If it is bad, you should have told us about it sooner," I told her. Had she been unwell all this time and we hadn't known?

"It's not bad. It just means I'm getting my—"

Her face and neck turned a delightful shade of pink. Even after everything we'd done to her, all the ways we'd claimed her body, she could still be embarrassed.

"Your courses?" Tor asked.

Three very focused, slightly worried faces stared at our mate as she nodded.

"It's not that," I said, certain that she was carrying our child.

"It's too fast for me to be pregnant. It takes at least two weeks to know," she insisted.

"As for too fast, that might be true on Earth, perhaps." I ran my hand over her still flat belly and thought of how it would soon be round. "On Viken, it takes four months from breeding to birth."

Her eyes flared wide. "Four months?" She placed her hand over mine.

"That means—"

"That means we go to the doctor."

• • • • • • •

Leah

"You have done very well, Leah, allowing the mentors to believe you are resisting us. Despite how things appear, they are all quite… forgiving, as they want every Viken bride to be fully satisfied."

Satisfied wasn't the word I'd use to describe how my men had pleasured me. Overwhelmed. Dominated. Protected. Cherished. Loved…

"The physical exam, however, is… different." Drogan glanced down at me as he led me toward the medical hut. It was larger than the others and set well back in the trees.

"Different?" Apprehension slowed my steps, but Drogan's hand on my elbow kept me moving forward.

"Your body will be truly tested and analyzed. The doctors and mentors need to ensure that any problems between us are caused by mental limitations, issues of trust, and not physical maladies. They can accept that a new bride has a fear of her mate, or is not used to fucking, but they won't accept a poorly made match or an undiagnosed medical problem. Remember, I am being tested by them as much as you."

"What do you mean?" I asked as we stopped outside the door.

"A mate must guide his bride. If I do not pleasure you, if I do not cherish you, care for you and earn your complete trust, then I am at fault."

Drogan tipped up my chin. "The medical exam is critical.

We will be scrutinized. You will be pushed, prodded, and tested. Here, I do not believe your resistance will be feigned."

On that ominous note, he opened the door and led me inside, dread slowing my steps as I followed him inside. The only thing that kept me from bolting was the knowledge that none of my mates would willingly put me in harm's way.

While no other couples had been in the various training huts we'd visited throughout the week, the medical center was definitely different. I froze just inside the doorway of the one large room, my mouth open. In one corner, a woman stood with her dress pinned up at the back, exposing her bare bottom. It was mottled red from an obvious spanking, but also horizontal stripes crisscrossed the obviously tender skin. She'd been spanked not only with a hand but with a belt or cane or... something. Her hands were up and behind her head and with her elbows flared out, she had to lean forward to touch her nose to the wall. This, of course, thrust her punished bottom out into the room.

A man who was probably her mate, along with another in a uniform, stood nearby and talked of her disobedience and a several-day plan to train her. I flushed at how they spoke of her as if she were an... object.

"Good, Alma, good."

The voice had me turning my head. A woman was on her knees sucking on a man's cock, which was hanging from the front of his pants.

"Keep your head still. I will fuck your face as I wish." The man's hand cupped the back of her head and held the woman still, her mouth stretched wide around his thick cock.

"You said you were concerned about her gag reflex." A man in uniform stood perpendicular to the couple and watched with detachment. "Show me."

The man thrust his hips, pushing his cock almost completely into the woman's mouth. Her hands came up and she pushed against her mate's thighs as her eyes widened. He held still for a second, then pulled back, but not completely exiting her mouth. The woman took deep breaths through her nose and she relaxed.

"Yes, I see. Her response is quite strong; however, it is not a medical problem, but a training one. I will tell the mentor to provide you with a training cock that she can practice on. You will want her to use it as you are fucking her so she can find pleasure—even come—when her mouth is full."

The man pulled his cock from his woman's mouth and used his thumb to wipe at her lips, his eyes full of admiration and... pride. While I could see the woman was humiliated at being discussed so brazenly and clinically, she also reveled in her mate's attentions, even more so when he helped her to her feet and kissed her forehead.

As he buttoned his pants, the man said, "Thank you, doctor."

The couple came toward us and we moved out of the way as they left. The doctor approached us and then shook Drogan's hand.

"It has been a week and I felt it time to come in," Drogan said. "I'm sure you can understand the reason for our delay."

The doctor nodded. "Certainly. I have heard good reports from the various mentors about your mate's progress."

"Yes, she was quite resistant to being watched at first, especially when I feasted on her pussy, but she seems to have gotten over that concern."

I flushed hotly, remembering the way Tor had pleasured me so ruthlessly in the training hut, my legs tied open so I could not resist. But the heat climbing my cheeks was also caused by the way he talked about me. I wasn't a possession, but he spoke of me as one.

"I'm right here," I muttered, my eyes narrowing at Drogan.

The doctor remained silent, but one brow winged up.

"I have been working on her behavior, but it is a... struggle."

Drogan sounded as if he was working with an untrainable puppy.

"What punishment methods have you utilized?"

"Spanking, of course."

"Some use a mate's bottom hole as a sure way to maintain obedience."

I wanted to kill the doctor, but I assumed that would be taking the term *recalcitrant* too far.

Drogan slid his big hand down my back. "I'm pleased to say that my bride enjoys ass play too much for it to be considered any kind of punishment."

My cheeks burned then and I looked at the floor.

"Ah, yes, I remember you spent time with the ass-training mentor."

Drogan squeezed my side, perhaps in reassurance.

"She has a very tight hole. More stretching is required before I can take her there, but she is quite responsive to anal play. I look forward to how she reacts to my cock plundering that virgin portal."

I looked up at him and my mouth fell open. I wanted it too, but... geez.

"Let's begin the examination, shall we?" The doctor moved to a table that looked just like one in my gynecologist's office on earth. I stalled as I stared at it.

"Here?" I whispered to Drogan. "There are going to be *people* in the room while I'm *examined*."

The woman still stood in the corner, the two men remaining near her. Another man came and went. There was *zero* privacy.

"Doctor, my mate responds better to rewards than punishment."

Drogan turned to face me as his fingers gripped the hem of my dress and lifted it, higher and higher, until the fabric of my dress was hooked over his forearm. While I felt the cool room air on my lower legs, I was still covered to everyone in the room. His finger nudged my clit ring before sliding past it, over my slit, parting me, then easily slipping two fingers inside me.

I grabbed his forearms as I whispered his name, this time in need, not embarrassment.

Leaning down, he whispered in my ear so only I could hear. "I feel our seed deep inside you. Do you know what it does to me to know you've been marked?"

His voice, while quiet, was filled with his own desire. He was as affected as I, but he had to be the strong one. I could barely form a coherent thought, but I knew he was under scrutiny as much as I. He had to get me off to prove his dominance and I had to give in to prove I was his match. The way his expert fingers found my G-spot and began stroking it, that wasn't going to be hard. "You're going to come for me, then you're going to let the doctor examine you. Nothing else, all right?"

I let my forehead fall against his solid chest as I dug my fingers into his biceps. "Yes!" I cried. My orgasm was so swift that I didn't stifle the one word.

I was panting hard as I tried to catch my breath, to recover. Drogan slipped his fingers from me, let the dress fall back to the floor. Tilting my chin up, I watched as he licked my arousal from his fingers.

"There is no question, doctor, that the match is strong."

"None, indeed," he replied. "Your seed power is potent."

"So is my seed," Drogan told him. "I believe she is already bred."

I was too sated to be embarrassed and I was thankful for Drogan's hands holding me up, his body shielding mine from others.

"Shall I log this patient for you, doctor?" A man asked the question, although I couldn't see who it was. I had to assume it was one of the other men in uniform.

"No, thank you. I shall enter her data myself when I

finish here. If she is with child, as her mate says, there will be additional forms."

"As you wish," the other man replied. I heard his footsteps retreat.

"Shall I examine her now?" the doctor asked.

"Yes, however, external scanning only. I will have no other man touch her, not even a doctor."

CHAPTER NINE

Lev

"Well?" Tor asked, when Drogan and Leah returned. I'd used the bathing room to shower while they were gone and only wore my pants. My feet were bare against the wood floor.

Drogan held Leah's hand and she looked well pleasured and a bit shell-shocked. My brother nodded and an eerie feeling settled over me. It was as if my life was settling into place. A week ago I was in Sector Two, alone. Now I had two brothers who I respected, a mate, who I ached for, and a child coming.

"Under four months," Drogan confirmed.

Tor walked over and tugged on Leah's hair. While he did it gently, her head tilted back so he could kiss her mouth, then gaze at her intently. "This does not mean we will be any less rough with you."

I approached, placed my hand on her still flat belly. "He is correct. However, I doubt the spanking bench will be much use soon enough."

Drogan laughed. "I'm sure you'll find other ways," he replied dryly.

"I will try one of them right now."

Leah tried to step back, but Tor's hold remained. "You'll spank me now? Why?"

I saw surprise in her eyes, but also eagerness. She could not hide that she liked the power I wielded over her. She liked to be spanked, the pain of it, the heady sense of submission.

"Because I can." I stepped back. "Tor's cock needs your attention, Leah."

My brother released his hold and moved over to one of the dining chairs. He pulled it away from the table, spun it around, and sat down. As he undid the front of his pants, he spread his knees wide. Leah licked her lips when his cock sprang free and he began to stroke it.

I angled with my chin toward Tor. "Suck his cock, Leah."

Her eyes flared at the idea and she walked over to him. As she lowered herself, hands and knees on the hard floor, he shook his head. "Hands here." Tor patted his hard thighs.

A little frown formed on her brow, but she obeyed, leaning forward and placing her small hands where he commanded. I came up behind and tossed up her skirts, settling the material on her back. Scooping an arm about her waist, I pulled her back so her ass was sticking straight out and her head hovered over Tor's straining cock. With his thumb, Tor swiped at a drop of pre-cum and raised it to Leah's lips. She sucked it into her mouth and groaned.

I pulled back my hand and gave her a swift strike to her ass. Instantly, a bright pink handprint flared to life. She cried out around Tor's thumb.

"Suck his cock, Leah."

Tor pulled his thumb free of her mouth and grasped the base of his cock, holding it for her to take. Lowering her head, she opened her mouth and swirled her tongue around the flared head, then flicked at the large ring.

I swear I could feel that hot little tongue on my own cock

and I groaned. Drogan knelt beside her and slipped his fingers through her wet folds, playing. She groaned. As he stood to the side, I was able to bring my hand down again with a loud crack. It wasn't overly hard, but the sound filled the room.

"Take his cock deep, Leah," I ordered.

In almost greedy fashion, she bent her arms and lowered her head, taking Tor's cock deep into her mouth. When Drogan tugged at the plug in her ass, something she had acquired during her examination, she groaned again.

"I won't last if she keeps making sounds like that," Tor said, his hand tangling in her fiery tresses.

When Drogan pulled the plug free, the two of us watched as her ass remained open for us, the plug having worked well to stretch her wide. Her body worked to close back up and instead of allowing it, Drogan slipped his slick finger into her ass, testing her training.

"We can take her tonight. Would you like that, Leah?" Drogan asked, beginning to slowly fuck her with his finger, going deeper and deeper into her ass each time. "Would you like this to be Lev's cock instead of my finger?"

I spanked her again. "Drogan asked you a question."

She came up off of Tor's cock long enough to say, "Yes, please."

"I will spank you until you suck the cum from Tor's balls and swallow it deep. Since you've got our baby in your belly, his seed can go elsewhere now."

I began to spank her, not overly hard, for while I knew it would not harm the baby, I was nonetheless cautious. This was more about her knowing who was in charge than any kind of punishment. For while she was sucking Tor's cock and I was spanking her and Drogan's finger fucked her ass, she was the one with all the power. She was the one who brought the three of us back together, who would give birth to the future leader of Viken, who ruled our hearts.

Her ass was turning a pretty shade of pink and she shifted her hips and squirmed, pushing back on Drogan's finger.

"You may come, Leah. You may come while I play with your ass."

The connection we shared was incredible. This woman, this beautiful, smart, daring woman belonged to us. Understood us. Let us do these dirty, naughty things to her. And came for us.

Tor didn't last long—I hadn't expected him to, since we were like horny youths around her—so Leah came hard, her mouth full of thick cock as his seed coated her throat, filled her belly. She rode Drogan's finger and I watched as her arousal dripped from her empty slit.

We would take her now, again and again, not for a new ruler, not for Viken, but for us. *For her.*

• • • • • • •

Leah

One thing I quickly discovered about being pregnant was that it wore me out. Making a baby in nine months—I heard—was tiring, but I was cooking a kid in four months and it sucked the energy right out of me. I'd figured when the doctor had confirmed I was indeed pregnant, that he would know the sex of the child. But being a strange planet, at least when it came to day-to-day activities, the Viken race chose never to discover the sex of any unborn child. I didn't know the laws of Viken and whether a female could rule the planet, so I worried about gender.

My men seemed to be thrilled with their potent seed and their virility, for after I sucked Tor's cock, they carried me to bed and fucked me on and off all day long. It seemed that the seed power did not diminish with pregnancy. In fact, I was more eager than ever. So were the men, especially continuing to play with my ass, ensuring that they could take me all at once. I felt well prepared for Lev's cock in my ass, but I was a little apprehensive about being double penetrated. But they distracted me enough, waking me from my little catnaps by touching my body, watching as, almost before our eyes, my breasts grew heavy and fuller, my nipples enlarged and darkened, my belly began to take on a slight curve. It was almost crazy to watch something happen in a pace unfamiliar to me.

They were planning to form the mating union after our evening meal, but I'd fallen asleep. The last I remember was turning to my side and feeling the sticky essence of their combined seed making my inner thighs slick.

It wasn't gentle hands and soft lips on my body that woke me, but instead strong hands that gripped me and pushed me to the floor. I came fully awake by hitting the wood floor with my hip, a large male body covering me.

"What? Drogan!" I cried. I could smell him, the scent of the three of them very distinguishable, even in total darkness.

"Quiet," he hissed in my ear. The tone wasn't gentle, but commanding and I stilled.

I heard fighting, the sound of heavy feet moving across the wood floor. Not just Tor and Lev, but others too.

"Find her and kill them," the voice said. It was dark, deep and menacing.

I saw the sharp glint of Drogan's sword, held in the hand that crossed over me, shielding me and the baby from harm.

The sound of flesh hitting flesh, groans, the slide of metal out of a sheath filled the air. Drogan pushed me under the bed further, his body blocking me. The only way someone was going to get me was through Drogan, or crawling under the far side of the bed.

I saw the dark shadows of legs from my new position, one set coming closer. A grunt, then a painful, wheezing sound was emitted, then the body fell to the floor. All I could see was a black shape and I panicked, thinking it might be either Lev or Tor. Pushing against Drogan, I tried to get out from under the bed and help, but he was unmovable. I began to shimmy across the floor instead, further under the bed to go out the other side, but a strong, unbreakable grip on my hip kept me in place.

"Find her," I heard.

"Why take her alive? Why don't we just kill them all?"

I held my breath at the coldly logical question as my heart raced in panic. These invaders wanted to murder my mates and take me prisoner? Why? And where were Tor and Lev? Were they safe? Were they outside with a dagger through their necks or an arrow in their chest? I closed my eyes as pain washed through me in a wave so fierce and filled with rage I never would have believed myself possible of such intensity after just a few days with my mates.

But they were mine. *Mine.* And I could not bear the idea of them being killed.

"I need the child. Find her. Kill the men. Once she gives me what I need, I'll take care of her, too. No woman will run Viken. There will be *no* unification."

I wasn't going to lead Viken anyway! What was this crazy man thinking? I didn't understand that at all, but I was very clear about the dying part. He wanted to kill my mates, take my child, and kill *me* after I gave birth.

I would have panicked, but this traitor had to get through my mates first and I had faith in them, in their strength and their intellect. Surely they could outsmart these traitors? They had to. They couldn't leave me. Not now. Not ever. My heart wouldn't survive losing one of them.

More fighting, tussling, men grunting, cursing. I tensed but Drogan's steady hand kept me sane as we listened to the sounds of the fighting and the door slamming against the wall. I could see the brightening sky through the now open doorway, and a man's legs as he ran away.

Then another body fell to the floor a few feet from me. I turned my head away at the vision of his sightless eyes, the blood gurgling from his mouth and the spear protruding from his chest. I bit my lip and concentrated on the comforting touch of Drogan's firm hand on my hip, and his cold steel ready to kill anyone who came near us.

I tried not to breathe, afraid my shuddering would give us away in the sudden silence that filled the cabin.

"Shoot him down, Lev! Don't let him escape." I heard the rich, dark growl of Tor's voice and relaxed for the first time beneath Drogan's fierce hold. Relief poured through my body as I realized all three of my mates were unharmed.

"He's mine," Lev growled. I heard the whistling of an arrow, then a cry of pain, a thud as the running man's body struck the hard ground.

"Nice shot. All clear, Drogan. Is Leah safe?" Tor's boots walked to the edge of the bed and I reached out with trembling fingers to wrap my hand around his ankle, grateful to be touching him, to know he was alive and safe.

Drogan slid across the floor, pulled on my hip, and forced me to give up my hold on Tor as Drogan tugged me out from beneath the bed. He stood, then picked me up and settled me on my feet.

"Light!" Drogan called out. "Turn on a fucking light."

Footsteps, then the room brightened beyond the pale dawn and I took the opportunity to study my mates. Lev and Tor were both splattered with blood, but otherwise unharmed. Their eyes, however, were filled with a quiet rage I'd never seen before. That fire would have frightened me, but I knew it was on my behalf. That fierce anger protected me and kept me safe.

Drogan looked down at me as Tor came to stand beside him, his breathing ragged. Both ran their hands over me but it was Tor who demanded I speak. "Are you hurt?"

I wasn't paying them any attention, but looking for Lev, who stood silhouetted in the doorway. I wanted all of my mates close. I needed to feel their touch, to know they were all alive, and well, and mine. Lev must have sensed my need because he walked to me and ran his hand along my cheek as the other two continued to inspect me for injury. I leaned into his hand for a brief moment and our gazes locked. I let my longing for him, my trust in him shine up in my eyes. There was no hiding anything, not from these men with their fierce loving and dominant hands.

Lev touched my lips softly before turning away. In a matter of moments his long strides carried him out of the hut and onto the grass.

"Leah," Tor said, his voice insistent. "Are you hurt?"

I shook my head. "No. I'm not hurt."

"The baby?" Drogan asked, placing a hand on my belly.

I put my palm on top of his and took a moment to listen to my body. "Fine. But what… what happened?"

Lev called from outside and Tor picked me up in his arms.

"I can walk," I muttered, but rested my cheek on his warm chest, glad to be held. My adrenaline seemed to have melted away and I was becoming weary.

Tor stepped over a body and he turned my head into his chest, covering my gaze with a firm hand. "Don't look, Leah." I didn't fight him, simply relaxed in his arms and listened to the steady beat of his heart under my ear. A feeling of warmth and safety settled deep in my bones. I'd never felt this content, not one single day of my life before coming here, to Viken and these warriors who had claimed me as their own. I didn't just have one strong mate to protect and care for me. I had the three strongest men on the planet. The reality of their power, their strength poured into me and I settled my hands over my belly, truly happy for the first time. I was carrying their child, a magnificent amazing child. And these men would watch over and protect my baby as fiercely as they cared for me.

While Tor stopped just outside the open doorway, Drogan went over to stand beside Lev. In the brightening dawn I could see the body on the ground, an arrow lodged in his side; it was the doctor.

Why did he want to kill my mates? Why would he betray his own people?

• • • • • • •

Drogan

I was a warrior. I'd seen death firsthand, friends and foes alike. I'd killed some men myself. Blood was certainly on my hands and I was jaded and hardened to such danger. Or so I thought. When men stormed into our hut, knives glinting in the double moonlight, fear pumped through my veins. I wasn't worried for me or my brothers, only Leah. She was innocent and pure, and carrying our child.

I would protect her with my life. So would my brothers. And we had. But it had been others who had died. Squatting down beside the first man, I rolled him over. Blood seeped from the protruding edges of the knife Tor had used to pierce his heart. Tor wouldn't have let the man live, nor did he believe a man should suffer before death. His thrust had been exact, efficient, and swift. The man hadn't even seen it coming. Two more were like that, and a third had a broken neck.

That one was all Lev. He was deadly with a bow, but seemed to take a certain fierce pride in his ability to rip a man to pieces with his bare hands.

I followed Lev across the grass and to the man lying panting on the ground. I recognized the sounds of pain, of fear. Anger. He rolled from his side and onto his back to look up at us. An arrow pierced his side, just below the ribcage. He would not live long, not because of the wound, for it was easily treatable in the medical center, but because I would kill him once we had the answers we wanted. The doctor dared harm Leah. He would die.

"Why did you do this? Who are you working for?" I asked.

He narrowed his eyes. Sweat coated his face as his hand gripped the arrow where it entered his body, his fingers coated in blood.

He laughed, pain etching the sound. "Only those who want to see a better Viken."

Lev angled his head toward the hut. "Those men, they're

dead. You're dead next."

"My death means nothing."

"Then who should I kill?" I asked, squatting down beside the doctor. The sky was quickly brightening and the dark crimson of his blood was a striking contrast to the grass on which he was sprawled.

"Me." We whipped our heads up to the voice coming from the woods.

It was Gyndar, the regent's second in command. He was not meek, or quiet, or unimposing any longer. As he walked toward us in the flowing white robe worn by kings of old, a very modern blast gun pointed at us, it all made sense. The regent's plan, the attack on Viken United, the assassination. Gyndar wanted power.

"We got in your way, didn't we?" I asked. I tried to remain calm, to keep my hands from clenching into fists when I wanted nothing more than to walk over to the bastard and break his neck. Surely Lev was thinking the same thing. While I wasn't surprised to see a weapon on the man, it didn't fit the image I had of him in my mind. Gyndar seemed more the sort to hide behind smoke and mirrors, to make others do his less than savory work for him. Thus, the doctor was dying in the grass while Gyndar walked free.

"I just had to wait for the old man to die." He offered a nonchalant shrug.

"But plans changed."

He gave a curt nod. "Yes, plans changed. It would have been simple if you had taken a Viken bride, easy to sway one sector against the others. But a matched bride and your mutual cooperation? That ruined everything."

I didn't know where Tor had taken Leah, but I hoped it was far, far away. If Gyndar showed his face, that meant he wasn't alone. Surely there were more enemies in the woods. Waiting.

"And then we disappeared." I needed to keep him talking, to give Tor a chance to take Leah to safety.

"Correct, but I have supporters everywhere." Gyndar

glanced down at the injured doctor. "Everywhere."

So, our plan to hide Leah had been working until the medical examination. Our concern over Leah's health was what brought the danger to her. Stupid. We should have sent for my personal physician from the sector. I trusted him with my life. If we'd been more careful, we wouldn't be in this situation.

"Where is your lovely mate? I'm afraid I need her to come with me."

"No," Lev said with finality. "We are taking our mate to Viken United where we will jointly rule until our daughter is old enough to lead."

I glanced at my brother. His eyes flicked to mine as he continued to taunt our enemies. "The baby's a girl, isn't it, doctor? One of your men—before he died—let slip that he wouldn't be ruled by a woman. He wasn't referring to Leah. He was referring to the *one true leader.*"

A girl. We were going to have a girl. If she looked anything like Leah, the three of us were in trouble. My fists clenched now. How dare this man put both my mate and my *daughter* in danger?

Gyndar made a simple gesture with his fingers and the men I knew to be hiding stepped out from the woods. There were at least ten of them, well-armed and prepared to kill us all.

Gyndar nodded to one man who was two steps ahead of the others, their apparent leader. "Kill them all and find the woman. I need her alive."

"We will see you in hell," I growled, leaping toward the man who would destroy my family.

CHAPTER TEN

Tor

I had to drag Leah away from the scene playing out before us. I place my hand over her mouth and dragged her back, farther into the cover of the trees as she fought me with all her might. Apparently, being tossed onto the floor and shielded by Drogan as Lev and I fought the men who'd come to kill her hadn't been enough to scare her. My heart swelled with pride at our mate's fierce spirit even as I knew I had to drag her away from the coming battle.

With blades slicing through the air, along with men's fists, it hadn't been the time to work out the details of who was attacking us in the hut, or why. It all became clear when the doctor had been discovered as part of the group. The thought that a man entrusted with the health and well-being of so many brides had tried to kill our mate made me sick. But not as angry as the knowledge that Gyndar wanted to steal our child and kill us all.

I grabbed her about the waist, my hand over her mouth and carried her as quietly as possible around the side of our hut and into the woods. I was in warrior mode, but that didn't stop me from reveling in the feel of her breath against my palm, her heartbeat against my forearm, the soft weight of her. They proved that she was alive and safe. I was used to fighting the enemy—the two men I killed lay dead on the floor of our hut—but now I had a more important job, keeping Leah safe. Lev and Drogan would deal with Gyndar. They could focus on this menace and trust me to keep our mate safe.

As I reached the cool shade of the trees, I didn't put her down, only lifted her carefully into my arms and whispered in her ear. I did not know how many men Gyndar brought with him, but I doubted he had revealed all of them. I doubted we'd killed even half of his assassins. "Remain silent."

"But Drogan and Lev!" she whispered, her eyes wide and etched with fear, not for herself, for my brothers.

Heat spread in my chest that had nothing to do with lust and everything to do with the softness, the genuine worry I saw in her eyes. If she loved my brothers, surely there was also room in her heart for me.

"Don't argue with me. Have faith, love. They are warriors, not pompous politicians who grew up wearing robes." I smiled down at her, amazed by her strength of spirit. "Be silent. They are trusting me to keep you safe, Leah. Don't argue."

She nodded and didn't fight me again as I shifted her into a more comfortable position in my arms. She didn't cry out as I carried her away and I was amazed by the calm set of her beautiful face. One minute she was asleep between us, the next she was under attack, learning that the Viken regent had been murdered for personal and political gain... and she was next. She was truly the *only* person on Viken who could waylay Gyndar's plans. If my brothers and I were dead, the child she carried was the man's only completion for power. Sure, Drogan, Lev, and I could unite forces and lead, but the various sectors wouldn't stand united as we desired—as the regent had wanted—without the future leader that was the physical embodiment of all three sectors.

The one true heir.

My daughter. Our daughter.

With Leah better settled in my hold I was able to sure-foot it over fallen logs, rocks, and stumps and veer toward the water's edge. Lev wouldn't be the only one who doled out spankings in this family. When it came to her safety, she obeyed. No doubt she would listen better after her ass was turned a bright shade of pink.

Her fear was not unfounded and I worried for my brothers. They were outnumbered. I'd seen Drogan about to tackle Gyndar to the ground when I carried Leah away. To her innocent eyes, it looked as if two of her mates were surely going to die. While I didn't know my brothers much better than she did, I knew how they were raised, how they could fight and what they were fighting for. They would survive and Gyndar would be annihilated.

In the meantime, I would get her to Viken United, to neutral ground, to the home that stood empty and waiting for us.

· · · · · · ·

Leah

It seemed that Tor was just as skilled at paddling as his brother. I was carefully placed in a small boat, one similar to the one I arrived in, and Tor took us back to Viken United. Once we were out on the open water and he was sure we weren't followed, he told me of our destination. I fretted the entire time over Drogan and Lev, the doctor, and seeing Gyndar—the man I recognized from when I transported—in a completely different light. He wasn't the second-in-command any longer. He wasn't a wallflower. He was intent on stealing my child and killing me, eliminating all of us.

Yet my mates were taking him on. As worried as I was for them, I was also proud of my warriors. They were the true rulers of Viken, and when faced with a deadly threat, they had united and fought as one. For me. For our child.

While Tor assured me of his brothers' wellbeing, I fretted quietly for hours until the stress of the day wore me down and I fell asleep. I didn't remember anything after that—arriving back in Viken United, being carried to Tor's parents' palace, or being put into a giant bed. I awoke to an empty bed, but when I sat up I saw Tor writing at a large desk. He put his work aside and came over to me. While I was very much naked, he was freshly clothed.

"How are you feeling?" he asked, his hands raking over my body. While his touch was far from sexual, I couldn't help but react. My nipples pebbled and my skin flushed warmly.

"Better now. I… I worry for Lev and Drogan."

He tucked my long hair behind my ear, eyed me intently. "They are here, unharmed."

I looked over his shoulder, but they were not in the room.

Tor smiled. "They are eating their morning meal and bathing. They promised they would come to you as soon as—"

The door opened, halting Tor mid-sentence. In strode my other men, clean, smiling and whole.

I scrambled off the bed, uncaring of my nakedness, and ran over to them. Lev scooped me up in his arms and held me close. I breathed in his familiar scent as Drogan came to stand behind me. I felt his hard body down the length of my back.

"Miss us, mate?"

"You know I did." Relief washed over me as I knew they were well and safe. "Gyndar?"

"You do not need to worry about him any longer." Drogan's voice was a deep growl by my ear. I spun around and he pulled me into a hug. "We will announce to the planet later today that you are our mate and that you carry the rightful heir to the Viken throne."

I felt skeptical. "That's all? You just have to tell the people and they will follow along? Aren't there more doubters like Gyndar out in the sectors?"

Drogan loosened his hold and I stood between him and Lev. Tor came up beside me and I was surrounded. Sheltered. Protected.

"Probably," Lev said. "This is our parents' home. The home that has been ours all this time, waiting for our return. Regent Bard had the right of it. The three of us should have come together sooner to unify the planet."

"Our parents died trying to unite the sectors and it is our turn now to return the planet to the old ways. We will stop training our men to fight each other and send them out to battle the Hive for the Interstellar Coalition, to protect us all." Drogan said. "Our actions this day will speak far louder than any words. Gyndar's betrayal will be broadcast to the entire planet along with our message. None will dare oppose us, for we each have staunch allies in the sectors, people we trust. The planet will thrive again, and all because of you, mate."

Tor's hand wrapped around my waist to cup my slightly rounded belly. Our child was growing quickly. "They will see your body round with our child and know that our words ring true, that this child, this daughter of ours, will be the new ruler in her time, with three powerful sector leaders to guide her and teach her what is right."

"You will tell all of Viken about our daughter now?" I asked.

All three men shook their heads. "Not now. Later."

"You have a punishment coming first." Tor picked me up and carried me over to a chair, where he shifted and moved me so I lay across his lap.

I tried to wiggle off his lap, but he was very insistent keeping me in place. His leg hooked over mine and a hand stroked over my belly. "This may be the last over the knee spanking for a while."

"I don't need a spanking," I huffed.

"I told you to be silent and you spoke as we fled the hut. Your safety is tantamount and you put yourself in danger."

"I was worried about my men!"

Drogan and Lev squatted down so they were level with my face. Lev stroked my hair behind my ear. "I am pleased me to hear your words, Leah, but Tor is right. We entrusted him with your life and your disobedience made it more difficult for him to keep you safe."

"You will receive a count of ten," Tor said, stroking his hand over my bottom.

"Then we will complete the mating union," Drogan added. "We can't tell all of Viken that we are a family if the union isn't official."

"And I want to breach this virgin ass of yours." As Tor spoke, he slid a finger over my pussy and up to circle my back entrance. With my arousal coating his finger, he nudged the tip inside of me and I clenched down on it. "You like that idea, don't you?" he asked, one second before he brought his other palm down on the curve of my bottom.

I startled at the surprise of it, but it wasn't overly hard.

"Count, Leah," he said.

"One," I replied, staring at Drogan and Lev.

"I only wanted to know you were safe," I told them.

Smack.

I sucked in a deep breath. That one was harder. "Two," I replied through clenched teeth.

Drogan's eyes flared with something, not heat, more like love. "We know, but it's our job to protect you. It's *your* job to protect that baby of ours."

Smack.

The baby. God, if I'd been caught or hurt, the baby would have been hurt, too. I had only thought of them. I hadn't thought of what we'd made, of the person growing inside of me. The little girl. "I'm sorry."

"We can't take care of her like you can," Lev added. He kept his hand on my face, cupping my jaw. His thumb stroked over my cheek and wiped a tear away.

Smack.

"Four." I was crying. "I'm sorry," I whispered. "I didn't think. This baby, it's… it's so new. I had no idea I'd have three men that I feared for. I didn't know I'd have a baby inside me."

Smack.

"Then this will help be a reminder of your new life," Tor said. "How many?"

"Five," I whispered.

Smack.

"This will be a reminder that you have three men who care enough about you to spank your bare bottom when you need it. To fuck you when you need it. To love you."

"All the time," Drogan added.

The idea of being loved by all three of these men made my tears fall unbidden. They slid down my cheeks and onto Lev's fingers.

"I love you, too," I said, sobbing.

Tor struck me again and again over different parts of my body, but I didn't count any longer, only lay wilted and crying over his lap. When he was all done, he stroked his hand over my tingling, hot skin as Lev wiped the tears from my cheeks.

"All done," Drogan said. "Letting us take care of you is going to be hard for you, Leah, but you *will* do it." He was adamant about the last.

"Even though Gyndar is gone, that doesn't mean there won't be other threats, other dangers. You will make this daughter for us while we take care of you."

He and Lev looked at me with such earnestness that I had to smile, albeit a watery one. The three of them could keep me safe *and* rule the world. They could do anything… except make a baby. And that was now my sacred duty in this family. A daughter.

Something powerful and wild flared to life inside my heart and I knew that until this moment, my daughter hadn't been real to me. Now she was, and I loved her with a fierce protectiveness I'd never experienced before, not even with my men. This was different. This child was mine and I was hers. I'd die for her, kill for her, and do whatever I had to do to make sure she grew up healthy and happy.

"All right. I agree. I won't argue with you again. Our daughter must be protected."

"Good girl, Leah." Tor's hand slipped down over my pussy. "She's soaking wet."

A growl followed as he lifted me up and carried me to the bed. I didn't have a chance to see if the others followed, for he kissed me, sweetly, carnally, and darkly. His tongue slipped inside my mouth to tangle with mine and the heavy weight of him, while most of it he held off of me with his forearms, felt like a safe cocoon of protection. I was safe. I was desired. I was loved.

Tor broke the kiss and sat back on his haunches. The other men were stripping off their clothes, letting them fall to the floor.

"We will stay here, Leah, in this house, with you, for the rest of our lives," Tor said, his hands stroking over my body, as if learning it for the first time.

"Here?" I asked.

Drogan nodded as he lifted his shirt over his head, giving me a perfect view of his flat stomach, rock-hard abs, and narrow waist. "This is where we will rule. With you. With our daughter."

"Brothers, let's make her ours, first." Lev was the first one naked and as Tor moved off me to remove his own clothes, Lev moved into his place. "Let's get you ready for us."

Leaning down, he took one pert nipple into his mouth and suckled. "Soon, we will take milk from here. Taste your life essence. As we gave you our seed, you will give us this."

I had no idea why the idea of having the men suckle at my milk-swollen breasts made me hot, but it did. Perhaps it was seeing Lev's head there, the feel of his wet tongue licking me, the pull of his mouth.

Finally, Lev lifted his mouth from my nipple to explore the soft side of my breast, Tor across from him and Drogan settled between my thighs. All of them had their hands on me, stroking, caressing, learning.

I lifted my hands to touch them, Lev and Tor's silky hair, the strong muscles of their arms, their smooth sides.

"This is right where you should be, Leah. Between us," Drogan said, meeting my gaze from between my thighs. His warm breath fanned my swollen, wet flesh. As I arched my hips, he grinned.

"Greedy, aren't we?" Only then did he lower his head and take me with his mouth. He tasted me, licking every drop of my arousal from my swollen folds, then circled my clit in very soft, very gentle strokes. When he slipped two fingers inside of me as he worked my clit, I came. Before meeting my mates, I could only come by touching myself. Now, I couldn't *not* come. I was so sensitive, so hyper-aware of them that I was multi-orgasmic. As I tried to catch my breath, I definitely wasn't complaining.

"Brothers, she's ready," Drogan growled.

They moved quickly, turning and shifting me as if I weighed nothing. Lev settled onto his back, propping himself up on a pillow. The other two lifted me up and onto him, my legs straddling his. With a firm grip on his cock, Lev lowered me down onto it, one eager inch at a time. He lifted and lowered me a few times until I was completely seated on him, my thighs resting on his.

I was so full that I groaned. "You feel *so* good," I murmured. My eyes fell closed and I placed my palms on his chest, just reveling in the feel of him.

"Then this is going to feel even better," Tor said, moving in behind me. He kissed my neck, then nipped the spot where it met my shoulder. "Lie down on Lev's chest. That's it. Good girl."

The men crooned to me as they helped me settle on top of Lev, my knees bent up and my breasts pressed into the springy, soft hairs on Lev's chest.

I felt a cool slide of liquid slip down over my back entrance. Tor's fingers stroked gossamer soft over that well-trained entrance, then slowly pushed within. I was thankful for the week of the plugs, although I certainly hadn't enjoyed them at the time. I'd had no idea how sensitive I was there, how many little nerve endings were awakened. Every time Tor's finger—or one of the many plugs—slid over that tender flesh, my arousal, my desire ratcheted up even more. I could come from anal play, but I wasn't sure I could survive a cock there. It was going to be too much, too big, too… intimate.

What I shared with my men was the closest I'd ever felt to anyone. All their attentions only made our bond even more intense. This… this was going to be insane. This mating union, I was almost scared by the rising intensity of it.

"Hurry, Tor. Her pussy's too good for me to last." Lev's voice was tight, as if he was barely holding on. Lifting my head, I saw the taut lines of his neck, the way his jaw was clenched tight. I could see the beads of sweat on his forehead, the effort it was taking him to hold back. His cock just rested deep within me, not moving.

"And I'm dying to get inside her mouth," Drogan growled as he stroked his cock. I saw a drop of pre-cum slip from the tip and slide over his fingers.

Tor slipped out of my slick back entrance and I felt empty, but only for a moment, for the slippery tip of his cock pressed inward.

"Breathe, Leah," Tor said, his voice close to my ear. One hand came down on the bed beside Lev's shoulder, the veins bulging along his corded forearms. The other lay on my stinging bottom and pulled outward, opening me up for him even further.

Taking a deep breath, I let it all out, allowing Tor to push forward. Even with all the plugs and just having his finger work the lube inside me, my body fought the new intrusion. His broad crown was bigger than any of the plugs and I was resisting. Tor's hand lifted, then came down in a hard swat.

"Let me in," he said.

I gasped and tightened my bottom, which only clenched down on Lev's cock deep in my pussy.

"She's fucking strangling me," Lev growled.

"Then she needs to let me in, or you'll come and we'll have to start all over."

"She'll get a punishment then," Lev promised.

It was hard to be outraged when I had Lev's cock in me. "You'd punish me for this?"

"Do not deny your mates anything, Leah, including that virgin ass." Lev said. "Push back and let him fuck you and fill your ass with his seed. *Now*."

The stern look on his face, the dark tone of his voice had me shivering with delight, yet also fearful of the punishment he might mete out. I *wanted* to let Tor fuck my ass, but it was hard.

I glanced at Drogan, who offered me a slight nod, then I placed my cheek down on Lev's shoulder, lifted my hips a tiny fraction and pushed back. As Tor forged his way forward little by little, I continued to offer my ass, tilting it up to him, presenting the last vestige of myself I hadn't yet shared.

I breathed through the stretching, the opening, the pressure of his cock until I felt a pop and he was in. Just the huge head, but he was in. I groaned, feeling not only Lev's cock, but now Tor's as well. Inside me. Opening me. Stretching me. Completing me.

"I'm in," Tor snarled.

"My turn now." Drogan moved closer to me. "Up, Leah."

I lifted my head, came up on my forearms so his cock was just in front of my mouth. The ring was big and shiny, the little hole at the center oozing more and more of his pre-cum. The color of his cock was a dark plum, angry veins pulsing up the long length. His musky scent was carnal and I licked my lips, eager to taste him.

God, he was going to come in my mouth. The last time that happened, I came, hard, screaming my pleasure. The same happened every time they fucked my pussy. I couldn't *not* come because their seed, God, their seed was so... amazing. I craved it. My body needed it. What was it going to be like when I had all three of them coming inside me at once?

My body softened at the idea.

"She just got so wet. It's time to move," Lev commanded.

Drogan moved closer and I opened my mouth for his cock. I didn't lick the head, didn't play with the ring. I opened for him and he pushed into me until his cock hit the back of my throat. Over the past week, my gag reflex had lessened and I'd learned to breathe through my nose. I could taste his pre-cum on my tongue, feel the way it made me hotter, more eager for them.

As Drogan began to slowly fuck my mouth with his turgid cock, Tor inched his way into my ass. Beneath me, Lev pulled back as he did so, then they reversed—a cock sliding into my ass as my pussy was emptied, then reversed.

I felt Tor's hips press against my ass as he bottomed out in me. Their growls mixed with my moans of pleasure. I couldn't keep my eyes open. I could do nothing but give over to what they were doing to me. I was a vessel, their woman who took them in all my holes. At one time. I was the only person who could connect them this way, to make us all one person, united.

The baby in my belly was a culmination of this connection, a physical proof that my men wanted me and only me, that this bond was the perfect match.

I tried to cry out around Drogan's cock, but my cry was muffled. They used me, all three of them. They gave me no respite, not that I wanted one. I could feel their pre-cum coating my inner walls. My ass, my pussy, my mouth. I was lost, tossed and turned.

"I'm ready," one growled.

"Now," said another. I couldn't discern who was who. I didn't care. It didn't matter. They were one. *We* were one.

"Yes," the third said.

With that, they got faster and rougher, once, twice, then they pushed inside of me all at once. A cock embedded in my pussy. One in my mouth. One in my ass. All three cocks pulsing with their orgasms, the thick, hot seed pumping out of them and coating every inch of my openings, sizzling and marking me so that I came. I couldn't scream, I couldn't move. I couldn't even think. I felt the bond between us, their pleasure mixed with mine. I swallowed down Drogan's cum, gulp after delicious gulp of it before he pulled out. I felt the excess seeping out around Lev's cock, dripping from my pussy. Deep inside my ass, I felt Tor's cock spurt. My ass was theirs and I would beg for them to take me there from now on. It was so potent, so real, that I almost lost consciousness, only returning to myself as Drogan pulled his cock from my mouth, used his thumb to swipe the corner of my lips.

He fed it to me and I licked him clean.

Tor carefully pulled from me next, then Lev followed. I was empty now, yet slumped across Lev's body, the connection remained. Tor settled on one side, Drogan, the other.

"We must make the announcement now?" I asked, my voice slurred with weariness.

"Soon, but I want to revel in our connection. I can feel the mating union, can't you?" Drogan asked.

I could. I *felt* them. I nodded against Lev's chest. His hand stroked over my sweaty back.

"Whatever the future holds, we will face it together. Whatever our daughter needs, we will be prepared to give it to her. Viken will be joined, united, just as we are," Tor added.

I smirked. "Not *quite* as we are." I couldn't help but blush, still embarrassed by my brazen passion for these men, even after what we'd just done.

"You brought us back together, Leah. You are the person who will save Viken," Drogan told me. The other men murmured their agreement.

"I like that, knowing I helped." I bit my lip.

"But?" Tor asked, knowing I was thinking of more.

"But can we come together like we just did… again?"

Tor lifted me off of Lev's chest and onto his. He grinned up at me. "You like when we take you together?"

I gave him a shy nod.

He reached around and stroked over my pussy, then my ass, both slick with seed. "Are you sore?"

"The baby?" Drogan added.

"I'm not sore and the baby's fine. More, men, more," I begged.

"Our pleasure," Tor said.

"Yes," Drogan added. "Our pleasure."

And they showed me again how united we truly could be.

THE END

Printed in Great Britain
by Amazon